For Hilary Martin

DOCTOR WHO
TRIAL OF A TIME LORD
MINDWARP

Based on the BBC television series by Philip Martin
by arrangement with BBC Books, a division of BBC
Enterprises Ltd

PHILIP MARTIN

Number 139 in the
Target Doctor Who Library

A TARGET BOOK
published by
the Paperback Division of
W.H. ALLEN & Co. Plc

A Target Book
Published in 1989
By the Paperback Division of
W.H. Allen & Co. Plc
Sekforde House, 175/9 St John Street,
London EC1V 4LL

Novelisation copyright © Philip Martin, 1989
Original script copyright © Philip Martin, 1986
'Doctor Who' series copyright © British Broadcasting Corporation,
1986, 1989

The BBC producer of *Mindwarp* was John Nathan-Turner
The director was Ron Jones
The role of the Doctor was played by Colin Baker

Printed and bound in Great Britain by
Cox & Wyman Ltd, Reading

ISBN 0 426 20335 6

One

The softly lit oval courtroom was in recess; empty except for the Doctor and a guard. The Doctor stared moodily at the giant screen that dominated the courtroom. On that screen of the Matrix of Time he had already witnessed one past adventure; now he awaited the ordeal of having his latest activities on Thoros-Beta examined, dissected, judged.

The Doctor moved his head from side to side, trying to shake fragments of memory into a coherent whole. Nothing came, neither pattern nor sense. He saw, in his mind's eye, a huge rock; a pink ocean, Peri's terrified expression as he raised an arm to strike her. *Strike* her? Why? Why? Helplessly the Doctor tried to remember the crime that had caused the Council of Time Lords to snatch him out of time and place him on trial for all his lives.

Soon the second part of his prosecution would begin. How, the Doctor asked himself again, could he defend himself when he could not even remember the offence of which he was accused? 'Crimes against the inviolate laws of evolution,' the Inquisitor's clerk had intoned when reading out the charges. What did *that* mean exactly? The Doctor did not know. His attention was caught by a sigh of disturbed air as a panel opened to the left of the

Matrix screen and the squat figure of Zon, Keeper of the Record of Time, waddled into the chamber. Watching the fat shape straining against his cream uniform the Doctor thought the official looked like a dumpling. A dumpling immersed in the stew of time.

Zon bowed needlessly to the ornately carved wooden chair that sat in lonely prominence below the centre of the screen before ambling towards the battery of Matrix time control panels.

The clerk of the court and the jury members were next to appear, their wide collars of stiffened lace rustling like the giant butterflies of Genveron. As the twelve Time Lords seated themselves below the throne of justice, a sinister figure, dressed in funereal black, appeared through the Advocate's door.

The Doctor forced himself to make a cheery wave of welcome to his adversary. Pointedly the Valeyard ignored the gesture and went to his lectern and began to busy himself with reviewing his notes for the prosecution of the Doctor.

The scene in the courtroom was almost set with only one vital participant missing. After another minute, an august presence appeared, resplendent in the gold and silver robe of supreme Gallifreyan justice. Haughty and remote, the Inquisitor showed the sash of her authority to the court. Gracefully the Inquisitor acknowledged the respectful bows of all in the court noting that even the rebellious Doctor seemed to be lowering his head, though, in truth, the Doctor was staring at his feet in a desperate attempt to marshal his thoughts and had hardly noticed the arrival of the Inquisitor.

Attack, the Doctor thought as the supreme justice seated herself.

The Valeyard adjusted his black advocate's cap,

looking as gloomy as a messenger of death.

'Members of the Court, we have just witnessed another glorious escapade of the meddling Time Lord known as the Doctor.'

Before he could continue the Doctor was on his feet waving his arms wildly and advancing on the Valeyard.

'My lady, I ask that the court protect me from the abuse of the brickyard!'

'Sit down and shut up,' the voice of the Inquisitor cracked across the courtroom, sending the Doctor back to his seat like a crestfallen schoolboy.

'Thank you, Sagacity,' the oily tone of the Valeyard stung the Doctor into retaliation.

'Sagacity! Since when has "Sagacity" been used in a Gallifreyan court of law?'

'I am simply showing respect for our learned Inquisitor.'

'Creep!'

'Doctor . . .'

'I apologise, my lady.'

The Inquisitor pointedly turned to the Valeyard. 'May we be allowed to view some evidence?'

'Certainly, Sagacity. I wish to examine the record of the Doctor's last adventure. The one that he was engaged in when he had to be expelled from Time and brought before this court.'

'Proceed.'

The Valeyard motioned to the Keeper of the Matrix. The screen glowed into life and revealed another screen on which twin worlds were to be seen, first at a distance, then in sudden close-up before receding almost instantly into the far perspective once again.

'Whoops, missed!' exclaimed the Doctor's image on the

7

Matrix screen.

'Not again, we're like a yo-yo not a TARDIS.'

'Oh, shut up, Peri, anyone can make a mistake.'

'Missing your worldfall by a million miles is some mistake, Doc.'

'Mere bagatelle,' the Doctor said, flicking with nonchalance a co-ordinator vector switch. Nothing much happened except that on the TARDIS screen the two planets jumped half a million miles nearer to them. The colouring of the two worlds became more distinctive.

'Ugh!' Peri pointed at the smaller of two worlds, 'what a horrible mess of colours...'

'Mmm,' the Doctor glanced at the green, blue and pink blotches that mottled the garishly coloured world which now filled the screen. 'Seems all right to me.'

'Hmm ...' Peri said, looking at the Doctor's coat of many clashing colours. 'I expect you find that mish-mash of colour attractive, huh?'

'Not bad.'

'The other planet next to it, the normal-looking one. I don't suppose that's Thoros-Beta by any chance?'

The Doctor, concentrating on timing the final flip that would send the TARDIS to their destination, simply grunted out his reply. 'Alpha, that's Thoros-Alpha.'

'And we're headed for the other one, eventually?'

'Hope so.' The Doctor stood back after making final adjustments to the navigational co-ordinates. The TARDIS' driving column turned and rose up and down a dozen times then fell gracefully into repose.

On the viewing screen of the TARDIS nothing could now be seen but a vast expanse of ocean the colour of candy floss – the pink clashing against the horizon of an apple-green sky.

'I feel sick just from looking at this Thoros-Beta,' Peri said.

'I think it's rather attractive,' the Doctor said then turned away from the screen and began to peer about him.

'What are you looking for, Doctor?'

'That phaser, I know I put it somewhere safe ...'

'In your pocket?'

'No.'

'Doctor ...' Peri said in exasperation and began hunting through the debris that littered the floor of the TARDIS. Finally, behind a pair of Venusian lung clamps, she located the dangerous weapon that had caused them to travel through space to Thoros-Beta.

'Ugh!'

'What is it, Peri?'

'This thing feels nasty ... Sticky ...'

'Oh, that'll be from the blood of the dead Warlord. Bring it along, Peri, bring it along.'

'Doctor ...'

But her companion had already ambled away out of the control room and seconds later she heard the exit doors open.

Crossly, she followed, holding the phaser gingerly at arm's length from her.

If from a distance the planet had seemed a wild hotch-potch of colour, on closer acquaintance Thoros-Beta held a brooding menace that owed much to the precipitous purple mountains that rose steeply from near to the rocky shore on which the TARDIS had materialised.

'What a dump,' Peri said, surveying the shoreline then staring up at the bare cliffs that towered above them.

'Peri, can you see any vegetation?'

'Over there.' Peri pointed at a mass of creepers that intertwined into a tangled mass at the foot of a rock-face a little way from them.

'Are you sure this is the right place, Doctor?'

'Yes,' the Doctor said, surveying the coast first one way then the other.

'Doctor, there's no sign of life, none at all.'

'Never mind. Fancy a swim?'

'In that goo ... no thanks.'

'Pretty colour, though. So much better than the blue and green water on that Earth of yours.'

Peri thought of her home planet and experienced the longing that she knew could so quickly become homesickness. In order to stem the feeling she said, 'I can't get over the weirdness of this place.'

'No?' The Doctor took the phaser from Peri's hand and began to examine the strange weapon for the umpteenth time. 'This was manufactured here. I'm sure of it, Peri.'

'Oh, yes.'

'It seems to have a multiple function ...' Nimbly the Doctor's fingers began to manipulate panels and interlocking segments on the ornately tooled butt of the weapon. 'Mm. That must give a varying range of force projection ...' Peri watched the Doctor make an adjustment, then, to her consternation, she saw the phaser begin to glow and then release a blinding beam of laser force. As luck would have it, the force bolt beamed away from them and centred on a sizeable boulder that stood a dozen paces away.

'Doctor, look, the rock, it's melting!' Fascinated they watched the boulder start to return to its molten state. Before meltdown was complete, the moleculer structure shattered, showering the beach with burning fragments.

Fortunately none touched Peri and the Doctor but the flash of force had been a fearsome reminder of the potency of the sophisticated energy weapon that they had discovered on the barbaric world of Thordon.

Peri and the Doctor stared at the burnt patch of rubble where the boulder had been, then at each other.

'Quite advanced,' the Doctor said, turning a restrainer ring that he hoped was the safety mechanism.

'Is that all you can say? That rock ...'

'Yes. Yes ... don't be a scaredy cat, Peri.'

'Doctor, don't point the gun at me!'

'Sorry.'

Warily Peri pointed at the phaser. 'Are you sure that was made here?'

'Oh, yes. A dying warlord wouldn't use his last breath to lie.'

'Then where is everybody, Doctor?'

'Peri, if aliens landed in the centre of the Sahara desert, what impression would they receive of your home planet?'

'Oh, all right.' Peri moved away impatiently. The Doctor stayed where he was, staring thoughtfully at the jumble of rock and shingle that comprised the beach.

'Mm,' the Doctor said examining a chunk of rock. 'Soft ... bit like limestone ... chalk ... flaking.'

'Come on, Peri,' the Doctor said, striding along purposefully towards the jumble of blackened vegetation at the foot of the purple cliff.

Hurrying to keep alongside him, Peri soon lost her breath and was pleased when the Doctor paused and began to examine the incoming tidal currents of the pink sea.

'Look, Doctor!'

'What . . . ? Oh, yes.' The Doctor glanced only briefly at the horizon where Thoros-Alpha had loomed up above the horizon like a prodigious orange. Still the Doctor studied the flow of the now-churning water. Peri felt ill from staring at the turbulent pink surf and turned away. Was there a movement that had almost caught her eye or was it just her vision confused by the visual assault of the colour combination of pink jello and bilious green sky?

'Come on.' The Doctor was off again, heading directly towards the mass of what could have been burnt bracken. The fibrous brown mass glistened and reflected the green light of the sky. 'Is it alive?' Peri asked with a tremor of apprehension.

'No, just moisture, sea spray . . . see . . . let's move this lot and . . . come on, give me a hand.' Though the vegetation was dead it was still difficult to shift, but eventually enough was cleared to reveal an opening in the cliff face.

'A cave, had to be, rocks so soft and the tides so strong, there had to be caverns and bore holes,' the Doctor explained.

'What's that?' Peri pointed at a wisp of pink vapour that curled from the interior of the cave.

'Oh, it's only mist. Don't be such a cowardy custard, Peri . . . come on . . . let's explore.'

Peri watched the Doctor duck and disappear into the murky interior. There was nothing else for it. Peri drew a deep breath and ventured a first tentative step into the caves of Thoros-Beta.

Two

'Doctor ...' Peri called into the gloom of the cavern.

'Over here.'

'Ugh, what's that smell?'

'Seaweed, Peri, only seaweed sucked in by the tide.'

'Where's the light coming from?'

'Don't know, must be openings overhead.'

'Where are you?' Peri said, her feet slipping and sliding on the residue of seaweed on the gallery floor.

'Here,' said the Doctor reappearing just at that moment to help Peri maintain her balance.

'Why—' Peri started to ask but the Doctor raised a finger and began listening intently to a distant sound.

'What's—' Peri began again.

'That noise ...' the Doctor said, frowning.

'Just the tide, isn't it?'

'No. I don't think so, Peri, come on...' The Doctor started forward again.

'Just a minute!' Peri protested. 'Before you go haring off ... what are we looking for?'

'Remember what that warlord said on Thordon. Tell them to send more of the beams that kill.'

'What would that savage know?'

'Exactly, Peri, how would a bunch of skullcrackers like the Warlords of Thordon understand such sophisticated killing devices?'

'I dunno. Perhaps someone gave it to them.'

'Yes.' The Doctor looked hard at his companion. 'And we must find out how and why.'

Peri shrugged. 'What does it matter how they bump each other off?'

'Matter? *Matter?* 'Course it matters. It's a possibility I've often feared: an advanced culture manipulating the destiny of a less developed civilisation. If that's what's going on here it must be stopped!'

Peri did not understand the Doctor's vehemence. 'By us?' she ventured tentatively.

'Yes,' the Doctor said. 'Who else is there?'

Peri nodded. It had always been pointless to argue at such times. There was nothing else to do but try and pick her way through the semi-darkness in the wake of the Doctor.

The Matrix Keeper, at a sign from the Valeyard, stopped the playback.

The Prosecutor addressed the Doctor. 'Who else is there? Your very words condemn you, Doctor. I ask the court to mark such arrogance well.'

'Sorry?' The Doctor was genuinely puzzled about the point the Valeyard was attempting to prove.

His adversary shook his head as if the Doctor were a wayward child. 'You feel only you have the right to meddle but anyone else, according to you, must be stopped.'

The Doctor stared at the Matrix screen. What was about to happen? Rather than continue to argue with the Valeyard he thought it best to play for a little more time.

'You'll soon discover I made the right decision,' the Doctor said confidently. He settled back to view the action as if he were completely unworried. Only he knew how fragmented were his memories of what was about to be shown.

On screen the court saw Peri hurrying through the swirls of pink mist after the Doctor.

'Doctor ...'

'Shush!' He had his head cocked, listening to the low hum of what sounded like powerful machinery.

'Louder, I'd say, Peri, definitely louder ... must be somewhere nearby ...'

'What's that?' Peri pointed as a patch of mist cleared to show a large bulky cone.

'Ah. Could that be the source of the noise?'

The Doctor moved rapidly towards what seemed at first sight to be a warning buoy but as the duo got closer they could see it was something far more complex.

'Incredible,' the Doctor said. 'Sophisticated ...' Peri heard a sound of what could have been claws on stone. Spinning round she saw only swathes of billowing mist. Was it her imagination or did the pink fog seem more poisonous-looking than before?

'What is it, Peri?' the Doctor took out the phaser as a precaution.

'There was a sound of, well, like claws ... Doctor—'

'Oh, rubbish ... you're hearing things. Just look at this, it must be an auxiliary—'

Then Peri screamed.

'Peri?' The Doctor turned, saw the glistening, green suckered arm reaching round the terrified girl's waist.

Before the limb of the creature could tighten further the Doctor tore the clawed hand free. For a second he glimpsed a huge domed head centred with a basilisk eye, then he was engulfed by a foul-smelling rubber pancake that heaved against him; choking for breath the Doctor felt the frightening embrace of what must be a sea creature. Struggling to extract his arm the Doctor realised he was still clutching the phaser weapon. Under the pressure of the pincer hand the Doctor felt the phaser activate. There was a searing blast and the grip that had been crushing the life from him loosened.

The cry of the creature was heartrending. Horrified, Peri and the Doctor saw the suckered arms flail, the side tentacles wrap about the console column activating an alarm system that caused a klaxon horn to boom out a raucous warning note every thirty seconds. To this accompaniment, the end came for the strange life-form. The arms lost their grip, the side tentacles loosened and the torso settled on its stumps; the domed head, with its staring eye, slumped and the whole body-mass keeled over. A green ooze spread from its mouth. The pincers on the end of each arm opened once, twice, then finally snapped shut.

'Horrible,' Peri said. Her voice trembled in the aftermath of shock.

The Doctor gazed down at the phaser in his hand. 'I thought I'd put the safety catch on.'

'Good job you hadn't.'

'Not for him,' the Doctor said, indicating the lifeless body at their feet.

'Why did he attack us?' Peri had to yell above the alarm system that blared out every thirty seconds.

'I don't know. Perhaps it was to protect this.' The Doctor indicated the auxiliary console.

Peri cupped her hands around her mouth. 'Shouldn't we get out of here!'

'Not yet, this must be a device for extracting energy from the sea ... but it's not the main regulator, there

16

must be a master control somewhere.'

The klaxon ceased its hooting.

In the sudden silence Peri looked at the fallen creature then at the tidal regulator.

'Was that thing looking after this?'

'Maybe, but he certainly didn't build it. Let's go and see if we can find who did.'

'Just a moment!' a disembodied voice cracked through the mist.

Startled, Peri and the Doctor turned towards the sound.

'What . . . ?'

'Over here.'

A man of medium height, dressed in black uniform, appeared out of the mist. He carried a phaser weapon of a similar design to that held by the Doctor. The officer was joined by two other uniformed guards, one of whom raised a hand and pointed. 'Officer Frax, look!'

The officer looked beyond Peri and the Doctor to where the dead creature lay sprawled in a pool of green blood.

The effect on Officer Frax was extraordinary: expressions of shock, grief, then anger twisted his face and mouth. He spat out one word. 'Murderers!'

'Wait,' the Doctor said with alarm.

Frax levelled his phaser. His companions followed his lead.

Facing the three deadly phasers, Peri panicked. 'That thing attacked us!'

Frax spoke evenly, his emotions now held under hard control. 'The Raak was not programmed to attack. You must have threatened him.' Frax turned his attention away from Peri and the Doctor for a moment and spoke to the guard on his left. 'Bring a carrying sling.'

'Officer . . .' The guard left quickly.

'All we did was land here—' the Doctor began.

'Where is your submersible?' Frax interrupted.

'Further along the shore.'

Frax nodded, regarding the Doctor coldly. The phaser still pointed at the second button of the Doctor's multi-coloured coat. 'You are part of Crozier's new group?'

'Oh, indeed, yes, of course.'

Frax relaxed a little and pointed at the corpse of the Raak.

'There will have to be an enquiry about his death.'

'We will help in any way we can,' the Doctor said. His voice sounding as sincere as he could possibly make it.

Frax seemed genuinely troubled. 'The Raak was proud of his upgrading. So happy to be in service to the mentors.'

'Do you serve them?' Peri asked.

'Everybody must,' Frax said simply.

'Ah, I see,' the Doctor said, then added, 'Pity the Raak lost his head and tried to squeeze Peri like toothpaste.'

'It was an accident,' Peri said gently to Frax whose sad gaze was only diverted from the body of the Raak by the arrival of the guard carrying a stretcher-like sling.

'Take him to the dissecting lab.'

For a moment the Doctor thought Frax meant him, but the guards shouldered past and began to lift the green creature on to the stretcher.

'If there has been a regression,' Frax continued, 'they will want to know why.'

'Quite,' said the Doctor. 'Of course they will.'

'You must come with us,' Frax said, 'we will take you to Crozier's laboratory. Once he has verified your identity you will be released.'

The Doctor nodded his agreement. 'Oh certainly, let's

do that. Security is so very important.'

'I'm glad you agree,' said Frax watching the Doctor closely while standing aside to allow his guards to carry the Raak past him. The Doctor's attention also shifted momentarily as the stretcher with its grotesque burden went by. In the second of his distraction Frax neatly removed the phaser from the Doctor's hand and politely indicated that Peri and the Doctor should fall in behind the Raak. With Frax bringing up the rear the party set off to meet the mysterious Mr Crozier. A meeting that could only deepen their implication in what Officer Frax had called murder.

Three

'Is the Transformer Helmet prepared?'

The handsome woman, known as the Matrona, checked the readings on the BTV scanning screen. 'Yes, Mr Crozier.'

'Let us begin,' Crozier said. A man in his late thirties, blond with pale almost colourless blue eyes, he possessed an abrupt manner that dismissed everything as uninteresting apart from his one consuming passion – that of how the brain functioned in any creature that had, or could be given, the power to reason.

His latest experiment lay unconscious on an operating table. A large muscular, fiercely bearded, warrior king from Thordon. Encasing his upper torso was a breastplate made from leather, studded with iron and decorated with a deep inlay of gold that betokened his royal status.

'Let us begin,' Crozier said, helping the Matrona to guide the helmet across the laboratory on its supporting arm.

'Slowly, Matrona, slowly ... what's ...?' A jewelled dagger had entangled itself in the pocket flap of Crozier's lab coat and had clattered to the floor.

'Barbarians,' Crozier said. His voice sharp with contempt as he guided the brain transformer towards the skull of Yrcanos.

The helmet closed on the massive head. The power source was switched through and the lights of the input condensers activated and glowed, waiting to pass the waves of power that, when completed, would alter the warlike personality of Yrcanos.

Fussily, Crozier checked the instruments on the main visual display units. Satisfied, finally, he thrust his hands out before him.

'Decontamination box,' he ordered.

The Matrona held out the square metal box, lifted the seal to allow Crozier's hands to enter, then activated the particle bombardment which would cleanse the scientist's hands of contamination.

The bombardment stopped. Crozier removed his hands.

'Let us pacify the brain of the barbarian.' Crozier moved to the Control Function Codifier. In his eyes could be seen the intensity of his excitement.

Following the Raak, Peri found herself mesmerised by the lolling head and the staring eye that opened and closed with the swaying of the stretcher.

This, taken with the twists and turns of the tunnels, soon disorientated Peri completely. All she could do was plod on through the dank, rock-strewn passageways.

Finally they reached a junction of corridors. Down one lay what seemed to be a room from which light spilled. Above them a red warning light was activated.

'We must wait,' Frax said, pointing up at the light. 'Crozier must not be disturbed.'

'Oh, what a shame we can't meet him straight away,' Peri said with a sidelong glance at the Doctor.

'Yes, it seems a lifetime since we saw old Crozier,' said

the Doctor.

Frax stared at the Doctor, his expression showing suspicion. 'Old? He is young for a man of science.' He paused. Perhaps you should describe Crozier to me.'

'Certainly,' the Doctor said, 'but shouldn't we attend to the Raak first?'

'Why? He is dead.' Frax frowned.

'Oh,' said the Doctor. 'I thought he just winked at Peri.'

'Cheek!' Peri said, trying to support the ploy of the Doctor.

'No accounting for alien taste,' the Doctor said. His eyelid lowered a fraction in an almost imperceptible sign to Peri.

Frax examined the Raak who sagged back lifelessly when the officer touched him. 'Surely he is dead.'

'Not necessarily,' the Doctor pushed Frax aside. 'May I examine him – I am a Doctor.'

'Like Crozier?'

'Yes. Yes. A colleague. Nurse Peri, please prepare to apply the skedaddle test.'

Peri swallowed nervously. 'Is that wise, Doctor?'

'The alternative might be quite nasty. Come round here, Nurse, quickly, before it's too late.' The Doctor, as he said this, picked up the Raak's claw as if trying to locate a pulse. 'Hold this,' he ordered as Peri joined him.

Trying not to grimace too much Peri took the pincer in her hands, which allowed the Doctor to manoeuvre so that Frax and the guards were on the opposite side of the stretcher.

'Ready to apply the test, Nurse?'

'More than ready, Doctor,' came the tense reply.

'Count of three then.'

Bending over the Raak the Doctor counted calmly,

'One and two...' Then, roaring out '*three*!' he overturned the stretcher with the Raak on to the guards and their officer.

In the confusion of his sudden action Peri darted away. But soon she heard footsteps gaining on her. She glanced behind and saw with relief that the Doctor was almost within reach of her, though puffing and panting with exertion. A solitary force bolt streamed by but after that a curve in the tunnel protected them from further fire.

Left behind, Frax restrained his men from going in pursuit. 'Leave them to their fate.'

The guards looked puzzled until Frax added, 'They are headed for the lair of the Lukoser...' There was no need to add anything. The guards grinned and nodded.

'We'll take our time, then go and collect what is left of their bodies.'

The rock out of which the passage had been blasted was rough-hewn. The Doctor rested a hand against the wall, trying to regain his breath. He was puzzled as to why they had not been pursued. Perhaps the mist which once more had swirled in had helped their escape but it was still perplexing.

'Doctor, what's this?' Peri offered a long white bone with jagged edges for his inspection. 'There's a pile of others ahead; what is it?'

'Not quite sure. A shin bone, no marrow... pointed, jagged edges...' Watching the Doctor examine the long bone, Peri remembered another adventure and did not wish to take part in a repetition.

'Let's get back to the TARDIS,' she said, then stood transfixed as the piercing howl of a soul in torment was heard from close by. The sound throbbed, reverberated, penetrated their hearing and upset that part of Peri's mind where unnamed terrors lurked. She turned to run, but the Doctor gripped her arm.

'No,' he said, firmly. 'Let's find what made that dreadful noise and why.'

'I don't want to, Doctor...'

At that moment the patchy pink mist cleared momentarily. 'Doctor, straight ahead, I saw something!' Peri's voice cracked with tension.

'What?' said the Doctor, alarmed.

'A shape... a... there!'

The Doctor strained his vision and just made out a vague shadow. 'A man?'

Peri blinked in surprise. 'Alone?'

'And unarmed, let's hope. C'mon!' the Doctor, clutching the shin bone, took a few cautious paces forward.

Peri followed the Doctor, then realised a vital factor. 'Doctor, whoever... whatever it is, he's chained to the wall, look!'

The head of the Lukoser lifted. Wild bloodshot eyes stared at them from out of a once-human face that had elongated into the muzzle of a wolf. On his bare torso large patches of fur grew at random. The slavering mouth opened, revealing long canine teeth, while from his throat came a rolling growl that made the hairs lift on Peri's neck. At the same time compassion made her somehow want to reach out to this hybrid creature, in chains and so obviously in torment. Impulsively Peri bent to him, which was a mistake for, alarmed by her sudden movement, the Lukoser snarled, gripped her arm and opened his fearsome jaws, aiming to savage her throat.

'Help me!' Peri managed to gasp out before the

Doctor looped both of his hands over the neck of the Lukoser, holding the shin bone as a lever against the throat of the Wolfman causing him to choke and loosen his grip on Peri enough to allow her to scramble clear.

The fur-covered paws of the Lukoser gripped the bone and forced it away from his throat. Exerting a strength that was beyond that of his attacker, the man-beast hurled the Doctor from him. Stumbling and staggering the Doctor began to run with the Lukoser bounding after him howling with anger.

Just as it seemed that the Doctor must be brought down by the snapping jaws the restraining chain reached its full length, causing a howl of frustrated anguish from the maddened Lukoser.

Peri went to help the breathless Doctor. 'Are you OK?'

'Yes... Now I am. Now I understand how that bone got its toothmarks...'

'What is he?' Peri stared in fascinated concern at the creature that glared, growled and panted just out of reach.

The Doctor considered. 'Looks a little like a man, acts more like a wolf... lycanthropy?'

'Man changing into a wolf. How?'

'Ask him,' the Doctor said without too much thought and was surprised when Peri took him at his word and stepped forward a pace.

'Good boy. Good dog. Nice man. Can you help us, we're—'

'Peri, be—' the Doctor started but before the sentence could be completed the chain tautened. The Lukoser twisted under its restraint and Peri was safe, a pace beyond the limit of the creature's range. Then an odd thing happened: instead of impotent growls and snarls and another attack, the huge jaws began to creak and stretch painfully in an attempt to form speech. With guttural croaking sounds the words slowly and painfully formed themselves.

'Uh. Hih-hel ... help ... muh ... me.' The great teeth gleamed in the semi-darkness while the long tongue formed the grotesque parody of human speech.

'Doctor ... he's crying ...'

The Lukoser, like a stray hound searching for an owner, sank to his knees before Peri and begged her for help.

So sudden was this change from savagery to docility that the Doctor and Peri felt secure enough to approach and comfort the unfortunate animal, but before they could reach him Frax and the guards appeared further down the passageway.

At the sight of their uniforms the Lukoser once more became a maddened wolf, hurling himself repeatedly against his chain, slavering and snarling in thwarted rage. After the first outburst of frenzy the Lukoser turned towards Peri, forced his jaws open and said, 'Go!' wagging his wolf's head in the opposite direction to that of the guards.

'Come on, Peri, do as he says.' The Doctor pulled Peri from the Lukoser who turned back to form a snarling barrier to any further progress by Frax and the guards.

Four

'Slow down, Peri... they don't seem to be following.'

Peri stopped her helter-skelter progress. 'I was thinking we should go back... that man... wolf... whatever... he asked for help.'

'We can't be certain.'

'He said "Help me...." Doctor, what is going on here? Sea monsters that seem able to operate machinery, a Wolfman that cries and begs us for help.'

'We'll find out,' the Doctor said, looking down the misty corridor.

In the distance a long mournful howl of anguish made Peri start involuntarily towards the sound.

The Doctor said gently, 'Not that way, let's find out some more before we know who we can help. Who we *should* help.'

Peri tried to close her ears to another howl even more heartrending than the previous cry.

'Who could keep a creature in such torment?'

'I don't know,' the Doctor said, listening to a sound from another direction. 'Someone's coming...'

'Which way?'

'That way,' the Doctor said, pointing in the opposite direction to where the howls of the Lukoser still sounded.

Peri's heart thudded. 'We're caught between the guards back there and whatever's ahead.'

Urgently the Doctor checked the rough, uneven surface of the tunnel wall. 'Nowhere to hide, try the other side.'

Frantically Peri scanned the wall then noticed a shallow fold that, given a lucky swirl of mist, might just hide them. 'Here, Doctor.'

They flattened themselves against the cold damp stone while what sounded like a small procession advanced steadily towards them.

'Can't you squeeze in a bit more?' the Doctor muttered.

'If you'd only lose some weight—'

'Shhh!'

Through the whirls of mist they could see the approach of a strange entourage of bearers and alien creatures that, to Peri and the Doctor, had a familiarity that they could not immediately place.

The first two mottled, green, lizard-like aliens were borne along on thronelike chairs held by carrying poles. The black-skinned bearers' muscles stood out as they trudged along with their burdens. When the third member of the trio came into view Peri gasped and only just suppressed her cry of surprise.

'Sil,' she breathed in astonishment.

The Doctor glanced at Peri warningly, worried that their old adversary might look towards their hiding place.

But Sil stared ahead haughtily, bobbing slightly under the progress of his bearers and soon disappeared into the pink vapour that seemed to permeate the underground caves of Thoros-Beta.

Peri stepped out into the centre of the tunnel and

looked up and down the mist-filled gallery. 'That was Sil, wasn't it?' she asked.

'Oh, yes.'

'How . . . ?'

'This is his home planet – didn't I tell you that?'

'You did *not*!' Peri's voice was hot with anger.

The steel-blue eyes of the Doctor looked innocently at his companion. 'What's the matter?'

'The matter . . . the matter . . . that Sil thing nearly turned me into a birdwoman the last time we met!'

The Doctor chuckled. 'How could I forget . . .'

'I want away from here – I mean it!'

The Doctor chose to ignore the problem and wandered a little way in the direction taken by Sil.

'Seeing Sil does explain one thing, Peri,' he said over his shoulder.

'Does it?' Peri's voice was still angry.

'Yes. Why disintegrator hand weapons came to be on Thordon. Sil would sell anything to anyone for a profit.'

'Can we go somewhere else?'

'Where?'

Peri glared at his back. 'Couple of galaxies further away from here would do just fine.'

'Don't be silly; c'mon, we mustn't lose track of your old friend.'

Peri watched helplessly as the Doctor walked briskly away from her; just as his figure was about to be enveloped by the mist her resolve to stay put weakened and with a scowl of surrender she chased after the Doctor before the fog could obscure him completely.

On the Matrix screen the all-pervading pink drizzle blanked out the screen which gave the Valeyard the cue to call a halt to the record of the Doctor's first foray into the underground tunnels of Sil's native planet.

'Do you relish danger?' the coal-black eyes of the Valeyard stared at the Doctor, hard and challenging.

'Not particularly,' the Doctor shrugged.

The prosecutor came from behind his desk. His black robes flapping behind him, a carrion crow who had spotted his next meal.

'Yet you court disaster so assiduously.'

'A Time Lord must appear to act with confidence at all times.'

'Even at the risk of his companion's life?' The questions put with the thrust of a rapier, stirred the jury. The Doctor replied as evenly as he could, 'He must risk his own life when necessary.'

The Valeyard closed in on his prey relentlessly. 'Already the unfortunate Peri has survived a struggle with the Raak, and escaped from the phaser fire of the guards. And who, Doctor, was sent to examine the Wolfman?'

The Doctor shrugged, which was a mistake that the Valeyard capitalised on. 'I'm sorry you treat the question with such indifference. I repeat, who was it went into danger first?'

'The one who happened to be nearest.'

The expression on the prosecutor's face was just the right mixture of concern and condemnation.

'Which happened to be your assistant – as usual.'

With a sudden dramatic turn the Valeyard addressed the august figure seated on the throne of justice. 'Sagacity, I have calculated, on a random Matrix sample, that the Doctor's companions have been thrust into danger twice as often as the Doctor has risked his neck.'

The Doctor came to his feet. 'There have been many companions but only one of me!'

The Inquisitor looked down at the prosecutor with a slight frown. 'What is the point you are attempting to make?'

'Simply this, Sagacity, the prosecution will later prove the Doctor to be an arrant coward. We will see his actions. I wish to make the point at this juncture that the Doctor has always been of a craven nature and statistics prove it.'

Waving his arms wildly the Doctor yelled out. 'This is the most preposterous travesty of a trial since the so-called Witches of —'

'Doctor, you have been warned.'

The ice in the Inquisitor's voice and the bailiff's move to produce a control baton made the Doctor swallow his anger. He knew that he could not argue about accusations, the details of which he could hardly recall. Dejectedly, he slumped back into his chair and stared at the screen that would reveal ... what?

'Proceed.' The Inquisitor turned back to the Matrix of Time which showed, at a touch from Zon, a setting that the court had not been shown before. A rectangular room that contained a puzzling mixture of exotic vegetation, running water from a central fountain and mixed up among the exotic shrubbery, an array of VDUs, computer banks and data processing machines that churned out reams of paper. A holographic projector brought to life miniaturised armies warring on a variety of worlds scattered throughout the universe.

'What is this, Zon?' the Inquisitor asked. 'Where are we now?'

The dumpling checked his coding indexes, then referred to the heavy Scroll of Record.

'It is logged as the Profit Room. Cosmic money and universal stock exchange.'

'On Thoros-Beta?'

'Yes Ma'am,' the Valeyard interjected. 'It is essential background for understanding the case, Sagacity.'

'Very well, continue.'

Sitting on the central control chair in the Profit Room was a small reptilian creature with a bulbous head that was joined to a yellow and black mottled trunk that tapered into a wriggling tail. Kiv's short arms had small, well-developed hands that were pressed on either side of his large, domed forehead.

'Marsh Minnow, master?' Another scrawny hand offered a glistening green newt to Kiv who declined the morsel.

Sil regarded Kiv worriedly. The leader of Thoros-Beta's Mentor class was obviously in pain. Sil decided to signal other lesser Mentors and the Thoros-Alphan bearers to hurry forward to Kiv's aid.

'Leave me!' Kiv's voice sharp with pain and authority halted the advance of his minions. His acid-yellow eyes rested on his assistant who was about to swallow another Marsh Minnow.

'Must you bring your lunch in here, Sil?'

Sil gathered together a small heap of slithering amphibians and conveyed half a dozen towards his mouth while conversing with Kiv. 'I do not wish to miss a moment of your infinite capacity to generate profit for Thoros-Beta. Are you sure we cannot share some Marsh Minnows, Magnificence?'

Kiv began to shake his head, then grimaced from the pain the movement caused.

'Let us get to work.' He turned to a data screen and began to scan the projections, prices and contracts on the futures market of the universal stock exchange. 'This

Thordon world. We must negotiate with the Krontep King. Usual contracts, development loans, some limited scientific advance. What is the position regarding King ... King ...?'

'Yrcanos.' Sil began to chuckle as he visualised the treatment that was at that moment being inflicted on the warrior king. 'He is still being "persuaded" by Crozier to co-operate happily with us.' Gurgles of grotesque laughter began in Sil's throat. 'I think "persuade" is the word for it, Magnificence!' Then Sil's laugh burst from him and the wild sound drowned the play of the water fountain and the busy electronic patter of the technology in the Profit Room.

Huddled over a probe screen, the Matrona and Crozier watched the process of pacification progress through the brain of King Yrcanos. Fascinated, they watch the slow dissolution of the warlord's braincells. Then, inexplicably, the process began to slow. The Aggression Locator seemed to be experiencing a mysterious resistance within the deep recesses of the warlord's neural network.

'Blood! Death! Terror! Kill! Skaadanwick!' Yrcanos bellowed each word as he fought the battle within his mind. The giant hands with their thick fingers twitched under the conflicting signals received from his besieged brain. Crozier was the first to react as the King reached for the pacification helmet and began to try to wrench it free from his skull.

'Increase the pulo pulse immediately!'

The Matrona scrambled to do his bidding. Though the pulse imput increased markedly and the Alpha waves decreased, still the warrior struggled against the power that surged through his brain cells.

'Samcnanz ... Cruz ... Craz ... Crome ... die ...!'

Worriedly the Matrona watched the muscles knot in the bulky arms.

'Why is the pacification not working?'

Crozier reached for an auxiliary power circuit and made a fine adjustment.

'It will now.' His dry voice was crisp and confident. 'Yrcanos is a barbarian King. He knows only one thing – how to fight. Therefore he is trying to resist our attempts to bring him to peace and tranquillity.'

'Scum!' the Warlord spat out, then succumbed to the process that Crozier had devoted his life to perfecting – the control and manipulation of behaviour.

Seeing the King at last made quiet, the scientist stretched his thin lips into a contemptuous half-smile. 'The stupider the subject, the longer it takes. Now, Matrona...' Crozier pointed to where an alien brain, the size of a water melon, lay open for dissection. Taking a slim stylus from the top pocket of his lemon-coloured coat he pointed to a stem of the opalescent mass. 'The ganglions have not yet recovered from the lesions of our last operation.'

The Matrona was an interested pupil. 'Why detach both junctions ...?' The sound of the laboratory door opening interrupted her question. Angrily she turned to berate the intruders.

'You are forbidden!' she began, then broke off as she saw the lifeless creature held between the guards. 'What ... what's happened ...?'

The Matrona moved across the floor of the laboratory but Crozier was quicker. 'An accident?' His voice was calm, detached, though the Matrona knew the disappointment the scientist must be feeling. The Raak represented one of Crozier's most notable experiments in alien brain enhancement.

'Answer!' the Matrona's voice was a whiplash that made Frax blurt out. 'Not an accident, murder!'

Crozier took in the word. It altered a lot of things. 'Whoever is responsible,' he said evenly, 'I expect their living brains to be delivered to me as recompense.'

Five

The junction of tunnels looked vaguely familiar to the Doctor as he edged round a corner warily. The red light glaring out above the door of Crozier's laboratory confirmed his impression that they were headed back in the same direction taken previously. Peri urged the Doctor forward.

'We're going in the right direction for the TARDIS, Doctor, keep going!'

'Wait ...' the Doctor warned.

'What?' Peri started to say, her voice bristling with impatience. 'Oh ...'

From out of the doorway of the lab came a funeral party bearing the body of the Raak. The group, comprising Frax, two guards, Matrona and a sad-faced Crozier, came towards the junction of passages where Peri and the Doctor were sheltering.

Already it was too late to run away with Frax and his guards almost upon them. Just as discovery seemed inevitable, Frax led his group away down the adjoining passageway.

'Let's get on,' Peri said with relief.

'No, not yet.' The Doctor paused looking down at the red light that seemed to draw his attention.

Soon the Doctor and his reluctant companion were

outside the laboratory. The Doctor pushed the circular steel door, which opened.

'Pooh!' Peri wrinkled her nose at the pungent smell that hung about the interior of the rectangular lab space. 'What's that, old socks?'

'Formaldyhyde, among other things,' the Doctor said as he stepped inside.

Peri followed. 'Wow – what's this, a pickle factory?'

'No...' the Doctor chuckled as they looked at the wall opposite where hundreds of brains, large and small, floated in jars of ethyl alcohol.

'Look...!' Peri pointed to an operating table on which the Warlord, Yrcanos, lay. Strapped to his head was a helmet dotted with an agglomeration of sensors and electrodes and a profusion of wiring that led to an assorted mass of technological paraphernalia.

While Peri moved to examine the unconscious warrior, her companion went to an oscilloscope on which an intertwining wiggle of amplification lines waved across the screen, tracing the electricity being sent through the patient's brain. Fascinated, the Doctor examined an array of neurotransmitters, nerve structure models, synapse locators.

'What *is* all this, Doctor?'

'Isn't it obvious?'

'No...!' Peri gasped at the arrogance of the Doctor's question.

On the screen of the Matrix the court watched as the Doctor excitedly began to trace the patterns of circuitry towards the helmet that encased the head of King Yrcanos.

'If I might beg the court's indulgence,' the Valeyard interrupted. The image of the Doctor froze in midstride.

'Well?' the Inquisitor turned from the screen as the scene dissolved into neutral grey.

'Sagacity,' the oily tones insinuated. 'May I be so bold as to suggest we have already seen enough.'

'I second that. The sight of that Sil creature would turn anyone's stomach,' the Doctor said flippantly.

A frown of annoyance flicked across the brow of the Prosecutor. 'We have now seen many examples of the Doctor's interference. We have heard the pleas of his companion to be taken away from danger. Yet again the Doctor has ignored her and gone blindly forward on his misguided mission.'

The Doctor spread his hands. 'Minor misdemeanours...'

The look on the Inquisitor's face became forbidding. 'You have asked for the penalty of death, Valeyard. You will have to show firm evidence as to why I should take such allegations seriously.'

'As you wish.' The Valeyard sat down, huffily.

It was the Doctor's turn to address the Inquisitor. 'My lady, for some reason I cannot yet fathom, I can recall little of the events on Thoros-Beta – neither my own actions nor the reasons why creatures like Sil acted as they did. May I see what the Matrix has to show, including all of the background material, so that I may see the truth of what happened to myself and why it is that Peri is no longer with me.'

The Valeyard jumped to his feet, his spare body trembling with rage. 'Preposterous timewasting. We will be here for months! And as for his oh-so-convenient loss of memory...!'

'Be quiet!' the Inquisitor regarded the accused and accuser thoughtfully. The time of her deliberation lengthened tantalisingly.

Finally, when the Inquisitor spoke, her voice was even and unemotional in her judgement. 'I will allow all Matrix material to be viewed by the court. To take all the lives of a Time Lord is without precedent. If that is to be the fate of the Doctor then it must not be said that the verdict for execution was reached without every effort being made to reach the truth.'

'My lady.' The Doctor bowed. He did not care for the references to execution but he was strangely elated. Now he would see what it was he had done. Good or evil, at least now he would know why he was here on trial and what had happened to Peri.

The screen of the Matrix glowed vibrantly once more and revealed not the scene of the Doctor exploring Crozier's laboratory but another location showing Kiv and Sil busily engaged in their Profit Room. Kiv was droning into a contract transposer. 'In the event of a major mining discovery, our lease from the Thordonians will be for thirty years at a royalty rate of forty per cent.' Kiv's large head lifted on a wave of pain. 'Or did I mean forty years at thirty per cent, Sil?'

'Thirty at forty is better, Magnificence.'

'Well, anyway, it will be enough to keep you in Marsh Minnows ... aah!'

'My lord...' Sil watched his superior rock to and fro in a vain attempt to escape the effects of brain compression.

'My head...' Kiv's mouth opened with the agony he was experiencing.

'It will soon pass,' Sil said.

The heavy head lifted wearily as the attack began to abate a little. 'The pressure grows worse each time.

Something must be done or soon you will be hailed as Magnificence.'

Sil looked suitably abashed at the awful prospect. 'Long may that day be postponed, great Kiv.'

At that moment the doors of the Profit Room were flung open. Horrified at the intrusion, Sil twisted on his water tank. The sight of Crozier and the guards crowding in caused him to escalate into hysteria. 'You must not enter the sacred room of commerce while profit is in progress!'

Crozier ignored Sil and addressed Kiv bluntly. 'There is trouble.'

'Concerning what?'

Crozier's grey eyes stared towards the leader of the Mentors.

'What has happened?' Kiv spoke quietly in contrast to the bombast of his assistant.

'The Raak is dead.' Crozier's tone was cold, his voice flat. 'Killed by intruders.'

Frax stepped forward. 'They claimed the Raak attacked them.'

Sil waved a short green arm imperiously. 'Then manufacture another experiment!'

Crozier gave him a look of utter contempt. 'That is not easily done. Neither is it the point of my concern.'

The Matrona spoke next. 'The Raak was no longer aggressive.'

'So?' Sil did not understand the problem.

Patiently, Crozier outlined his dilemma. 'If the Raak, unprovoked, did attack these intruders, then he might have regressed genetically. Until I know, until I can question the strangers in every detail, I cannot guarantee the success of your brain transference, Lord Kiv.'

'You must relieve my suffering!' Kiv's voice, at the

thought that hope of relief might be taken from him, had an edge of panic.

'My Lord...' the Matrona intervened. Sometimes only her soothing tones could calm the stricken leader. 'We have hopes that the radical treatment you require will be successful, Lord.'

Jealously, Sil attempted to block the influence of the Matrona's encouragement. Glaring at the scientist and his assistant, he adopted a hectoring manner. 'So much depends on the life of Lord Kiv. The making of mega wealth for the funding of your work, Crozier.' The little red eyes, buried in the green scaled face, gleamed when scoring this last point.

Crozier refused to be budged from his position of scientific objectivity. 'I must be certain. I must know that the chances of success in the brain transplantation are as favourable as possible.'

Sil turned his attention to the officer of the guard while Kiv once more hung his head as another surge of pain and nausea spread through his mottled brown head and body.

'Where are these strangers?' Sil asked.

Frax swallowed, he had feared this question, 'Escaped, Mentor Sil.'

'You, Sil, take charge!' Kiv's voice rasped out. 'Stupid guards, moronic bearers, incompetent officers! I will be dead as that Raak if I wait for them to find the intruders...' His reedy voice faltered with the anguish of further neural compression. 'Find them at once! Before I perish, then where will you all be? Huh? Leaderless and *poor*!'

Sil trembled at the prospect. He did not care too much about Kiv but the prospect of losing Kiv's mastery of stock-market manipulation galvanised him into action and soon he was spitting out orders that sent all available officers, guards and bearers scurrying in a desperate hunt for Peri and the Doctor.

'Ugh!' Peri turned away from a shelf that contained the pickled entrails of a giant swamp maggot. Next she stared through a magnifying panel that was focused on the open brain that had so engrossed the Matrona and Crozier an hour earlier.

While Peri wandered from one disturbing sight to the next the Doctor had been occupying himself in tracing the technology that was linked to the helmet enclosing the head of the inert warrior.

A movement on the operating table caught Peri's eye. 'He's coming round.'

'Not necessarily,' said the Doctor, engrossed in the complex combinations of neural formulae that flashed across the display panel of the electroencephalograph. There was much to understand in the pacification system, but finally the process began to make sense. The Doctor decided to take a calculated risk by lessening what he decided must be the power impulse into the helmet.

'What's going on, Doctor?'

The Doctor indicated a neural impulse passing across the oscilloscope. 'Not sure. But that brainwave belongs to that chap ... I've lessened the ...' Before the Doctor could finish, the door to the laboratory was suddenly thrust open. Peri and the Doctor turned to face half a dozen phasers held by black-uniformed guards who then stepped aside to allow a small green Mentor to be borne towards them by his muscular bearers.

'How nice to see a familiar mug again.' The Doctor smiled at Sil, then nodded a courteous greeting towards

Crozier who had entered immediately after Sil.

Sil smirked in satisfaction at his capture. 'Doctor ... and, ah, yes, your revoltingly ugly assistant.' He stared at Peri. 'Age has not improved you since Varos.'

Peri curtsied. 'From you, that's a compliment. What can we do for you, Sil?'

Sil scowled. 'Tell us why you had to murder our most promising experiment.'

'The Raak ...' Crozier interjected.

'He attacked us,' Peri said.

Crozier shook his head. 'That I doubt very much.'

An idea became blindingly obvious to Sil. It made him bounce up and down, forcing his bearers to brace themselves to keep their balance. 'Doctor, we have the means here to instill co-operation.' The stumpy fingers pointed towards the operating table threateningly. 'There is the technology that allows us to control the way brains think. Would you like to try the helmet on for size, Doctor?'

'Now just now, thanks,' the Doctor said.

'But I insist. Our warrior King must have completed his advancement cycle. You must replace him so that we may coax the truth from your devious brain. Take him!'

Sil motioned to the guards who grabbed the Doctor while the others assisted Crozier to unhook Yrcanos and lift him on to an adjoining table. Struggling, the Doctor was carried to take the Warlord's place. Strive as he might the combined strength of his captors was too much and soon the Time Lord found himself with the pacification helmet clamped on to his skull.

'No!' Peri tried to bar Crozier's way towards the impulse power switch but it was a futile gesture. She was pushed aside and the scientist made for the switch that would pour the power of the Cell Discriminator into the brain of the Doctor. At the last moment Crozier hesitated.

'Use the power!' Sil screamed across at him. 'We must find the truth of how they killed the Raak!'

'I've never tried the Discriminator for this purpose. It could well be fatal.'

'Never mind,' Sil said. 'Do it. I will take the responsibility.'

Crozier shrugged: he was exonerated by Sil's order. He turned the dial and depressed the CD switch. A wave line jumped to show that the current was being transmitted into the brain of the helpless Time Lord.

Peri cried out as the body of the Doctor convulsed with shock, her moans of despair drowned by the gloating cackles of laughter of Sil as the Doctor succumbed to the insidious invasion of his mind.

Six

The Doctor's legs kicked frantically as the Cell Disintegrator began to work on the network of personality structure within his brain.

'Stop it!' Peri shouted as Sil continued his wild outburst of manic laughter which was cut off abruptly by the sight of King Yrcanos sitting up with a sudden violent movement.

'Sanvanloomah!' The warcry startled Sil into a cowed silence. Yrcanos picked up a jar of preserving fluid and hurled it at the guards. Seeing Frax level his phaser weapon before discharging it into the Warlord's massive body, Sil yelled. 'Don't shoot, we need him alive to sign contracts!'

'Slug!' Yrcanos picked up the table and ran with it held horizontally before him, smashing the guards and Frax up against the shelves of sample jars and causing much debris and damage particularly to the unfortunates sandwiched between table and shelves with a bombardment of pickled brains falling upon them. Nimbly dodging the rush of the King, Peri ran to the transference panel and switched off the power to the helmet that enclosed the Doctor's cranium.

Crozier, horrified at the destruction of his beloved laboratory, watched helplessly as Sil screamed orders but cowered away from Yrcanos in a corner. Groggily, the Doctor began to stir.

Yrcanos stopped cracking the skulls of two guards together and called to the Doctor. 'Fear not, my friend I have had the brain purge and survived!'

Yrcanos turned his attention to smashing the brain transference system. Peri lifted the helmet from the head of the Doctor, then began assisting him to sit up.

'Where ... ?' The Doctor started; his voice was thick with confusion.

'Never mind. C'mon, Doc, let's get out of here.' With a minor explosion and a burst of sparks, Yrcanos yanked out a transformer and used its cable to swing an arc of destruction amongst his foes. Following in his wake Peri supported the Doctor and headed for the door.

They arrived as Yrcanos hurled a guard back among his fellows. 'After you!' Yrcanos allowed Peri and the Doctor ahead of him, then, with a roar of triumph, slammed the door and tied the cable around the locking arm with a quick flourish. 'Come,' he ordered and thrust out a brawny arm to help propel the Doctor away down the tunnel.

Inside the lab Sil raged at Frax and his defeated guards.

'Fools, fools, why didn't you fire!'

'You said ...' a guard started.

Sil pulled a phaser from the holster on the guard's belt, adjusted the force setting and pointed the gun. 'Could you not do this, stupid?'

Sil squeezed the trigger control. The bolt hit the guard in the chest. He somersaulted, hit the wall then slumped down on to the floor. The other guards shrank away from the angry Mentor.

'Don't worry. He isn't dead. And even if he was there

are plenty more oafs available from Thoros-Alpha! Creditless cretins, leave him and get that door open!'

Sil gave out the orders authoritatively but inside he had a sickening feeling that Lord Kiv would demand a reckoning for this latest blunder.

'Can we rest for a moment?'

'All right.'

Yrcanos propped the still barely conscious Doctor against the wall of a silent empty tunnel then immediately went off to explore. Peri tried to rouse the Doctor by slapping his face on either side.

'Doctor!'

'Uh?'

'It's Peri...'

'Yes,' came the dull reply. 'So far away ... up above myself on the table below.'

'Open a vein, let out the evil those devils have put into him.' The deep voice of Yrcanos growled from behind them. Having completed his scouting foray he had returned to stare down at the Doctor.

'Sorcerers! Evil demons! Soul stealers! They have my equerry, Dorf, in a dungeon somewhere. We will release him or die in the attempt! Were you captured by the slugs who rule this ball of mud and slime?'

Peri nodded.

'What we must do,' Yrcanos said casually, 'is kill all who stand between us and victory. We'll grind every last Mentor beneath our heel, yes?'

'You've got the wrong idea. I just want to get away. Not go slug hunting.'

'We must raise an army and attack the oppressors!'

The bellow echoed back and forth between the walls of rock.

'Sure, anything you say,' Peri said hastily in an effort to stop Yrcanos from bringing every guard within earshot running to recapture them.

'Good.' Yrcanos squatted down to address the Doctor. 'Don't worry. Your mind will clear. We will pile up the heads of our enemies before us like melons in a heap.'

The Doctor's eyes opened wide. For the first time since his rescue a glimmer of animation came into his eyes. 'I would like that.' His voice was gloating and filled with relish at the thought.

Peri could not believe the Doctor's obvious enjoyment of the barbarous image.

'*What?*'

Yrcanos nudged Peri and pointed at the Doctor. 'I like him. We will campaign together. Now we must march. What is his name?'

'The Doctor.'

Yrcanos stood back and saluted her with an upraised arm. 'I am Yrcanos, King of the Krontep, Lord of the Vingten, Conqueror of the Tonkonp Empire, but you, no doubt, know of this.'

'We caught some of it. About round seven. When you began using cell disintegrators on each other.'

'What?'

'Phasers.'

'Oh.' Yrcanos regarded Peri from his towering height. 'Your name, rank and title?'

'Well, er, Perpugilliam of the Brown.'

'The Brown, eh. Where is this Brown?'

'Earth. You'd like it there. They'd probably elect you President of somewhere.'

'Of course.'

'Yeh. You'd do well in politics.'

'Politics?'

'Yakkity yak. Talk.'

'War councils?'

'Yes. No. I don't know or want to know.' Peri began to find Yrcanos and his concentrated gaze disconcerting.

'I would wish to meet the mighty warriors of Earth.'

'Well, good luck.'

'You are promised to such a one?' Yrcanos posed the question with a surprising delicacy that took Peri by surprise.

'Me?'

'Are you promised to him?' Yrcanos turned a giant thumb in the direction of the recumbent Doctor.

'Certainly not!'

This statement made with some vehemence seemed to please Yrcanos. He stroked his beard, rippled his muscles and slammed a fist against his breastplate with a resounding thump.

Peri decided the developing interest of the warlord should be diverted quickly. 'I, er, must . . . must help the Doctor . . .'

She knelt down and began to shake the Doctor by the shoulder. 'C'mon Doc, wake up, please . . .'

On the Matrix screen the court watched Peri's hand move in close up to shake the Doctor. His eyes showed a glazed expression. The Valeyard made a sign and Zon held the image so that the Doctor's face loomed large above the court, frozen in vacuity.

'Doctor . . .' the Inquisitor addressed the Time Lord before her in the dock. 'Why did you begin to act differently on Thoros-Beta?'

'My lady, I cannot remember anything after the power was sent through my mind.'

The Valeyard strode into the space between Inquisitor

and accused. 'That is your defence is it, Doctor? Amnesia, forgetfulness? This is a tactic, Sagacity, because the Doctor knows what the Matrix must show...'

'Enough, Valeyard. Doctor, is that your defence – amnesia?'

Tousled blond curls shook in confusion. 'I thought I could recall what happened on Thoros-Beta.'

The Valeyard laughed. A sound that contained no trace of amusement. 'You are in for a surprise Doctor, an extremely nasty one if your memory is as fallible as you pretend.'

'What surprise?' the Doctor was genuinely curious.

'I prefer not to spoil the secrets of the Matrix.'

'Do not bait the accused, Valeyard.'

The Valeyard bowed before the Inquisitor. 'My apologies.'

The Inquisitor looked enquiringly at the Doctor who was frowning with the effort of recall. 'Anything further to add, Doctor?'

Abstractedly the Doctor shook his head, looking a little like his image that still stared vacantly from the Matrix screen.

'Very well. Proceed.'

The screen switched abruptly back into the wreckage of Crozier's laboratory. Kiv and Sil watched Crozier trying to untangle a jumble of wires that had erupted from the Brain Transformer.

Kiv's dry testy voice grated out. 'We must have the Transformer operational; how can we rule without its influence?'

Crozier sighed impatiently. 'Everything will be restored before your slaves realise their situation.'

'Never mind them. What of my predicament? The

pain in my head increases.'

'Your brain will continue to grow until . . .' Crozier shrugged at the obvious conclusion to his diagnosis.

Appalled, Kiv stared at the scientist. 'What?'

'Your skull, Kiv, is not designed to allow for increase of brain size and power. That's the trouble with mutations and hybrids like you. Your cranium is too thick. It lacks elasticity, hence the pain.'

Kiv knew just what Crozier meant for at that moment the pressure within his skull was causing him increasing anguish. 'Yes . . .' he moaned. 'Yes . . .'

Crozier regarded Kiv coolly. 'Unless I can operate, you will suffer fatal brain compression in a few days at most.'

Through a film of pain Kiv tried to concentrate on the scientist whose knowledge alone might save his life.

'You were brought here to give me new life!' the voice of Kiv wavered reedily. Crozier began to speak to him as if to a backward child.

'The Doctor has the answers I need. If the Raak did attack, my intended experiment of cerebral transfer must also fail when attempted on you. You would enjoy a few weeks of relief then you would revert to the base instincts of whoever was the donor.'

Kiv could stand no more. 'Words!' he screamed. 'Excuses! This is a conspiracy to stop my life being prolonged!'

Sil, alarmed at his master's growing hysteria, began to babble a mixture of flattery and empty promise. 'The intruders will be caught . . . all I want is to share in the light of your intelligence and profit from its shining wisdom . . .'

For Kiv this rivulet of inanity was worse than Crozier's condescension. 'Enough, Sil, do you want to talk me to death?'

'I will pray to the Great Morgo for your immediate recovery, Magnificence.'

'You will do better than that. If the Doctor has the answer Crozier needs you will find him!' Kiv paused, wincing under the onslaught of another compression of agony. When it passed a peak he continued, 'You will find him or you will both share my death with me. I can only stand this suffering for one more day. One day, that is all you both have ...' Kiv gathered all his remaining strength and spat out a final imperative. 'Do something or die!'

Sil signalled for his bearers to lift him. 'We will act, Magnificence. Bearers, bear me away!'

Driven by Sil's panic the husky bearers charged enthusiastically for the door, causing a tidal wave inside Sil's tank.

'Not that fast, you Alphan oafs!'

The bearers slowed and carried the irate Sil away in search of the Doctor, while Crozier returned to the repair of his beloved consciousness adjustment and transference systems. Kiv watched him work for a moment than wearily indicated to his servants that they could convey him back to the Profit Room. One day, he thought, I can stand this agony, for one more day but after that, no more. After tomorrow all those who have failed me will be no more.

The decision made his spirits lift and Kiv leaned back and closed his eyes. The careful sway of his water tank soothed him a little. A memory came to him; a memory of his home mire before his brain had started to develop. He remembered how the awakening had commenced, how the world of swamp and slime had become not home and safety but just the mire from which every embryo

Mentor must crawl. When Kiv had eventually reached the caves of the Mentors he was welcomed by other mutant amphibians whose intellects and bodies had developed further into enlightenment than had his own. All Mentors were due to perish after a few brief years of brilliant acumen that wrested a living for their planet from the universal stock and futures markets.

Now was it his turn to die, Kiv wondered. Yes, unless Crozier could avert the fate of all Mentors whose expanding volume of brain came up against the restriction of an unyielding skull. Tomorrow would decide, Kiv told himself as the rocking of his carrying poles lulled him into a few moments of blessed sleep.

Seven

Peri had been staring at the huge back of King Yrcanos for what seemed like hours. They trudged on and on deeper into the caves. The Doctor stumbled along behind.

'Quiet,' Yrcanos held up a hand.

'What?'

'Listen...'

All Peri could hear was the slow drip of water falling somewhere within the shroud of mist ahead. Then the mist thinned as the glare of search lamps began to cut through the pink vapour.

'Back. Retreat, move!' Yrcanos shepherded Peri and the Doctor back the way they had just travelled until they reached a cleft in the rock that might hide them from the probing lights of a patrol of guards. Crouching down, Peri and Yrcanos realised that the Doctor was making little attempt to hide from the approaching lights of their enemies.

'Doctor...'

'Wha...?'

'Get down!' Peri pulled him down next to where Yrcanos crouched on the floor of the natural alcove. Light blazed above them but only momentarily – the sound of the guards' steps continued their progress without breaking stride.

When the patrol had gone, Yrcanos stepped out into the passageway and helped Peri to step clear of the rocks that littered the floor of the entrance to their hidey hole.

Slowly the Doctor emerged to join them, his eyes dull and devoid of his usual intelligence. Worriedly, Peri passed her hand before his unblinking eyes. Not a flicker of response came from her movement.

'Yrcanos, you must help me get the Doctor back to the TARDIS.'

'This is not the time to run away but to fight. We should follow the guards. Annihilate them one by one just as I did on my long march to Kronwart.'

'How? What with?' Peri demanded. 'We're unarmed!'

Yrcanos shrugged casually. Peri tried again, 'What would be the point?'

'Victory!'

A wolflike grin came to the mouth of Yrcanos. Placing a platelike hand on either side of Peri's head he stared into her eyes.

'I am the victor of 97 battles, 1008 skirmishes, none of them minor.'

Peri felt his hands begin to exert frightening pressure.

'Can you feel my power, my strength?' Peri tried to nod but that was made impossible by his powerful grip. A voice cut in. A voice dripping with sadistic pleasure.

'Go on, flatten her face, slowly, slowly...'

With a gasp, Peri realised the voice belonged to the Doctor who was trying to egg Yrcanos on to crush her skull for his entertainment.

Yrcanos laughed. 'Blood, Doctor, is that what you crave?'

'Yes, oh, yes. But do it slowly so that the victim feels the terror of an extended death.'

Peri yelled out. 'Yrcanos, don't add me to your victims!'

'Why not?' the Doctor urged.

The laugh of the warlord echoed around the gallery bounding back at them from the rocky walls.

'The Doctor thirsts for blood. Let us not disappoint him. Let's move.' Yrcanos released Peri and shoved her playfully towards the inanely grinning Doctor. With a guffaw the King strode off into the mist. In imitation, the Doctor pushed Peri ahead of him.

'You heard the King ... move ... !'

'Doctor ...'

'Move!' The voice of the Doctor was harsh and fearsome in its intensity. Frightened by the latest turn in her predicament Peri hurried after Yrcanos, not sure if she might not be safer with the warlike King than the increasingly treacherous Doctor.

A line of Thoros-Alphans, clutching their djellabas for warmth about them, shuffled along in a line that wound in a half-circle following the curve of the induction centre. They were waiting to be examined and assessed for suitability for labour in the service of the mentors. Black-uniformed guards watched the miserable line of men and women and children move towards the screening centre where an aged medical officer, Marne, sat at the controls of a body scanner that could assess the state of health of a body almost instantly.

'Next,' the Mentor said, his voice weary with boredom. Already that day he had dealt with 424 immigrants.

The latest scrawny specimen grasped the computer terminal rods under instruction from a technician. 'Mentor Marne, we are ready.'

'Yes, don't shout,' Marne had unusually sensitive hearing and the everyday sounds of life underground were often distressing to him. Marne extended a long index finger and pressed the key of assessment. The Assessor Unit buzzed and clicked busily before displaying data on its VDU. This was echoed by a ghostly metallic synthesised voice that intoned 'Reject – disease – renal incipient. Reject! Reject!'

Two guards hustled away the Alphan, pausing only to salute Officer Frax who had entered the area of the Induction centre at the head of a search patrol. Then it was the turn of Frax to salute, for, from another linking passageway, came Sil and his party. Meeting in the centre the leaders of the search parties began to confer.

There was a third entrance that led into the circular space that contained the Centre for Induction. Along this, drawn towards the light and activity, came Yrcanos, Peri and the Doctor.

Cautiously Yrcanos peered around the corner, taking in the line of Alphans, the guards and the patrols of Sil and Frax who had merged together.

'What's going on?' Peri tried to stretch her neck to see around the bulk of the King.

'They bring all new slaves here. But see, lady, those guarding them have weapons: liquifiers that we must obtain.'

'We? That includes me, huh?'

'On my planet a Warrior Queen fights alongside her King.'

'We're not on your world, Buster!' Peri's voice was almost as pugnacious in tone as his. A slow smile of delight spread across the broad mouth of Yrcanos. 'It does not matter. The same rule applies, come ...'

The Doctor seemed dazed again. He had propped himself up against a wall and stared across at the wall opposite. Peri could not decide what had more expression, that wall or the Time Lord.

'Come on!' A large hand took hers and pulled Peri into the light of the open chamber.

After the mists and semi-darkness of the caves and tunnels the glare seemed intense, but still the strong hand propelled her towards the line of Alphans.

The guards responsible for watching the immigrants had eyes only for the meeting of Sil and Frax who were involved in an angry exchange.

'Which corridors and tunnels have not yet been searched?' the voice of Sil carried across to the guards around the computer assessor unit.

'Ow!' Marne winced at the angry tones of his fellow Mentor. 'How can someone like Sil possess a voice that can both shrill and grate at the same time?' he asked plaintively of no one in particular.

'Everywhere has been searched,' Frax was saying in reply to Sil. 'Except for those outlets to the Sea of Turmoil.'

'Then search *there*, stupid!'

Frax motioned to his patrol to follow Sil's order. As the guards began to disperse Yrcanos prepared to make his move. Having taken Peri through the queue of immigrants the King was now within striking distance of a guard who had a weapon held loosely in his holster belt. Yrcanos glanced over his shoulder and indicated his target. Peri nodded in dumb assent. Then stealthily Yrcanos closed in on his quarry. Three steps away from his prey Yrcanos froze as a voice called urgently across the chamber.

'Look out, behind you!' It was the voice of the Doctor.

The threatened guard turned, saw the danger from Yrcanos and went to draw his phaser while another guard bravely ran to tackle the barbarian King. Easily checking the rush of the guard, Yrcanos then hoisted up his attacker like a sack of barley and hurled the unfortunate guard towards his fellows.

Vaulting over the terrified Marne, who sat with his hands pressed to his ears, Yrcanos made for the nearest exit, assuming that to be the direction in which Peri had gone. Instead, Peri had momentarily dropped from sight, having seen a phaser weapon fall to the floor during the chaos that ensued from Yrcanos hurling the guard across the chamber. She retrieved the phaser, then stood and levelled the weapon towards the guards who had started to regroup. Sil, halfway across to where the Doctor was being held prisoner, frantically made his bearers halt as Peri turned her attention towards him.

Everyone waited for Peri to make the next move. Praying that her voice would be strong and firm she called across to the Doctor. 'Doctor – come over here!'

'No thanks ...' came the reply.

'Doctor ... ?' the bewilderment was clear in her faltering reply.

'Charge her down!' Sil yelled.

Peri turned the panel on the phaser butt and pressed the activator trigger. Nothing happened. With guards rushing towards her, Peri threw the useless weapon at them and ran for the corridor down which Yrcanos had disappeared. The guards all hesitated, turning to Sil who was interested only in the Doctor. The latter smiled as his enemy approached him.

'Doctor, the pleasure of your company is, of course, infinite.' Sil paused to savour the moment. 'But why have you chosen to warn us rather than help your friends?'

The Doctor shrugged. 'The odds were against us. Why should I risk my life over a savage and a stupid girl?'

Sil slobbered; an expression of pure pleasure. 'So you betrayed your friends. How wonderfully wise of you, Doctor.'

'I think so.'

The chuckle in Sil's throat was one of satisfaction but his cunning deep-set eyes never left the Doctor's face.

'You are planning some trickery, of course. I remember you are most ingenious. This is a ploy, yes?'

The Doctor shook his head. 'Why should I follow a mad Warlord of Thordon. What's in it for me?'

'You prefer to live?'

'I'm no hero.'

Sil gloated and leered. 'I could have sworn you belonged to that stupid breed.' The mad laughter echoed around the cavernous chamber.

The Doctor did not join in but earnestly replied to Sil's observation, 'I don't wish to help anyone any more. Now I'm just like you, Sil.'

'How nice for you.' The Mentor turned to his guards, his voice dripping with satisfaction.

'Inform Crozier and the Lord Kiv that I, Sil, have captured the Doctor ... the turncoat Doctor, it seems.' Again the manic laughter spilled out. The Doctor licked his dry lips and stared shiftily round him, looking exactly what Sil had called him, a turncoat who had just saved his own skin by betraying his friends.

Eight

'The truth of what you really are can now be seen by all, Doctor,' the Valeyard's voice rang out while the Doctor stared unbelievingly at himself up on the Matrix screen.

'That is not me. I would rather be dead than live like that!'

The laugh of the Valeyard was harsh. 'Like so much of what you have said to this court, they are hollow words. What we have just witnessed is but a glimpse of your later treachery.'

'No!' the Doctor cried out in desperation. 'I must have suffered displacement of my reasoning faculties.'

'You were overcome by fear, Doctor. Your one aim was to escape unscathed. Just you only. Your friends did not matter.'

'Never!'

'You realise the Matrix of Time cannot lie?'

'Can't it?'

'I suggest you confess to your crimes and throw yourself on the mercy of this court.'

An ominous silence spread through the Supreme Court of Gallifrey. Miserably the Doctor stared around at the disapproving faces of his fellow Time Lords.

Maybe it was true, the thought entered the mind of the Doctor. Should he beg for mercy? No. No. There was

something wrong, he told himself. Something...
something... ah, yes, of course. The Doctor clutched at
a possible explanation. 'Sil was right – a ploy to fool the
Mentors. Yes, clever old me...' A wave of relief washed
through the Doctor's being. 'Let the Matrix show what
it will.' His right hand made a gesture of invitation. 'A
clever ploy, you'll see.'

The smirk on the face of the Valeyard was worrying to
the Doctor.

'Do you really believe that Doctor?'

'Of course,' the Doctor replied, boldly.

'Then let us see.' With a swirl of black gown the
Valeyard turned his back on the accused Time Lord and
strode back to his seat. With that irritating smile still
evident he leaned back and awaited the next segment of
the Matrix visual record.

The scene that appeared was set in the wrecked lab with
Crozier trying to mend the damage done during the
escape of King Yrcanos. The court saw a guard with a
phaser covering not only Crozier but a familiar figure
who was assisting the scientist in the repair of a Nerve
Impulse Modifier. With a shock of recognition the
Doctor realised that it was he who was helping Crozier.
The images on the screen moved around to allow Sil to
appear. His face muscles working in unison with the
clenching and unclenching of his hands he was obviously
in the grip of the darkest suspicions of the Doctor's
motives in offering to help Crozier and the Mentors. Sil
could contain himself no longer. 'I do not trust the
Doctor!'

The Doctor melded a transistor to a matching
terminal then straightened. 'What I have told you is the
truth. I don't lie, it is not in my nature.'

Crozier looked up annoyed that the work of repair was being halted.

'He cannot know our reasons for questioning him about the Raak, Sil.'

'The Raak attacked us, without warning.' The voice of the Doctor was sincere.

'I believe him. Now can I please be allowed to redesign the Behavioural Ultrasonic Input Codifier?'

'Do you have time?' Sil asked.

'Not really. The help of the Doctor might just make it a possibility.'

The dilemma of whether or not to trust the Doctor made Sil itch all over. 'Water me!' he yelled at his bearers, who hurried to their scoops and began to dip into the tank that contained the cooling liquid of Sil's home waters. The soothing balm on his dehydrated, scaled skin made Sil relax a little. He decided to share his worries.

'If the Lord Kiv dies, his bodyguards have instructions to destroy us. You must operate to save his life. Not only his – *ours!* There's no time for anything else, Crozier. You must operate and successfully, tomorrow!'

Crozier looked contemptuously at Sil.

'What else have I been saying?'

'What do you need?'

'You well know – a donor able to accept the brain of Kiv.'

'I will find you one!' Sil promised wildly, agitated at the awful thought that he might be experiencing his last few hours of precious life.

'I could attempt a temporary transfer. Someone with a suitable cranium size would give us a few extra weeks . . .'

'Right,' Sil started then stopped as the Doctor had begun fiddling with a jumble of wired electrodes.

'Is there a microcircuitry diagram?'

'Stop him, it's a trick!' Sil started to shout.

'What have we to lose? Let the Doctor help if he wants. Here ...' Crozier passed a programme disc to the Doctor.

'Be certain you are right, Crozier,' Sil began but the scientist and the Doctor were absorbed in the process of repairing the Brain Transposer.

'Do you have a module unit replacement or is this ganglion separator adaptable?'

'It's multifunctional, Doctor.'

'Good. The switches...'

'I'll try them...'

The display screen showed some basic data of plasmapheresia that had not been there before. Crozier and the Doctor looked at each other. Was there some hope of success?

'If we can get the Lexifier to function...' they both started the same sentence.

The sudden onset of co-operation irked Sil. 'I still suspect a trick...'

'Go and find me a donor, Sil.' Crozier said. 'There is a chance I might save Kil's life and ours if you find me a suitable head.'

'All right. I will search and if I fail we can always use the Doctor!'

Sil grinned and signed to his bearers. Before the door closed the Doctor heard Sil giving orders that two guards were to remain outside the laboratory. The Doctor concentrated on repairing the BTV, dutifully following the instructions that Crozier occasionally issued.

With the mist making a pink haze before her, Peri plodded on alone. She felt constantly on the verge of tears. Lonely and lost, she felt anything that happened would be preferable to the solitude of the dank gloomy tunnel. Eventually, after what seemed a very long march, she came to a series of chambers filled with electronic equipment that glowed and buzzed, busily fulfilling some mysterious function of Thoros-Betan engineering.

Wandering from chamber to chamber Peri felt a sense of shock when she saw a green-skinned Mentor sitting with his back to her. Before him lay a bank of monitors that showed various views and aspects of the shoreline of the pink ocean. Peeping into the room, Peri's eyes scanned the screens, looking for a clue as to where she might be. Her gaze rested on a screen that showed a familiar buoy-shaped auxiliary unit.

Peri recognised the point where she and the Doctor had battled with the Raak. Her eyes shifted to the next screen and saw herself from an angle of a camera above her in the corridor. The Mentor turned to her. Peri took a step backwards preparing to make herself scarce and cannoned into Officer Frax who, alerted by a signal from the Mentor, had come to investigate the alarm.

'I see you have discovered the heart of our energy supply,' Frax said.

Peri nodded. 'Very impressive. Although I should have thought it qualified for a guard.'

'As a rule intruders never reach this far but I will pass on your suggestion to the great Kiv.'

'Do that,' said Peri. 'And pass this on at the same time!'

'Ow!' Frax cried out as Peri stamped her foot down on to his.

Surprised by the sudden attack Frax moved a vital couple of hops away, allowing the girl the opportunity to dart away into the mist-filled passageway. Unknown to

Peri she was very near to the route that she had followed once before, for parallel to the course she was running, was the tunnel where sat the Lukoser.

Shaking his chain the Lukoser began to whine softly, a keening sound that rose and fell, sounding more human than canine. Hearing footsteps the Lukoser bared his teeth, crouched and prepared himself. This time, he thought, I will wait and pounce and rip and tear. A figure, wearing a breastplate, short fighting tunic, and a bristling black beard appeared. A growl started in the throat of the Lukoser but the sound quickly turned into a croak of recognition. 'Yuh... yo... your Majes... Majest...'

Yrcanos, seeing the animal rise before him, adopted a fighting stance, arms raised to defend himself. He stared into the wolflike face with dawning comprehension.

'Dorf? My equerry, Dorf... not you?'

The wolf head moved up and down in abject misery.

'What have they done; what!' Yrcanos bellowed, his roar of rage resounding round the tunnel.

'Huh... help me.'

'Yes, yes, yes!'

Yrcanos turned his rage on to the chain that restrained the Lukoser. The Wolfman also began to heave on the chain and under their combined strength the ring driven into the rock began to shift, then loosen and finally pull clear.

Yrcanos and the Lukoser embraced, pounding each other's shoulders and pausing only to look at each other. Finally, Yrcanos could contain himself no longer. His deep voice rolled out in a long vow of intent.

'We will kill the sorcerers who did this to you. I swear by the great jewelled sword of Krontep that you will be revenged! Come!'

66

Yrcanos strode purposefully away with his equerry loping along beside him.

Peri had heard the echo of the shout of Yrcanos and hope of finding him had made her retrace her steps, which almost brought disaster for she nearly ran into a group of marching guards. Hearing their steps she had time to turn, but the clearing mist betrayed her and Peri heard Frax shout, 'There she is!'

There was nothing for it but to run, although Peri felt she could not keep up any pace for more than a short distance of ground. Turning a corner she saw a small spill of light from under the closed door of a chamber. Taking a chance she reached the entrance, pushed against the door, which opened and she slipped inside. Behind the door a yellow silk curtain was draped from hangings above the frame. Peri, heart jumping, stayed behind door and drape, not knowing what was beyond the saffron curtain but realising that capture was imminent from the guards whom she could hear approaching from outside.

Frax gave an order to his men to halt outside the wooden door. Stepping forward he raised a gloved hand to push the door open. Yrcanos and the Lukoser entered the same passageway. Seeing the Lukoser at liberty panicked the guards. Without waiting for an order they began to open fire. Turning tail the Lukoser and Yrcanos evaded the phaser bolts and disappeared the way they had come. Meanwhile Frax and his guards broke ranks and set off in pursuit.

On the other side of the door Peri wondered at the shots being fired, but after a time the silence outside seemed to warrant her once more venturing forth.

As she reached for the handle of the door, the curtain

was pulled aside behind her and a woman's voice said, 'Don't go, not yet.'

Peri turned and came face to face with a tall confident woman.

The Matrona no longer wore the cool white of the laboratory coat but a vivid crimson gown. At her throat a circular gold collar highlighted the tones of her rich brown skin.

'You're from the Induction Centre? Rejected, running away?'

'What?' Peri did not understand about the Induction Centre but after the Doctor's betrayal the rejected part sure made sense. The Matrona looked Peri up and down approving of what she saw. Her manner softened. 'I should inform the guards – have you returned to Thoros-Alpha.'

'Should you?' Peri's manner was polite but she really had little idea what the imposing woman was implying.

'There's an alternative?' A slow smile hovered on the Matrona's wide handsome lips. 'You were brought to serve the Mentors and their favoured creatures. I control the woman servants. I need help to do that. Loyal help.'

'I'd serve you. Why?'

'I prefer some individuality in my household. I like a small number of my personal maids to be unprocessed, you understand?' Peri didn't but nodded anyway. The Matrona took this to be a sign of agreement. 'Should you be discovered as an escaped reject, I will deny all knowledge of this meeting. What is your name?'

'Peri.' She should have offered an alias but it was already too late.

'Do you wish to serve me, Peri?'

The clatter of returning guards outside the door decided her. 'OK. What have I got to lose?'

'You must address me as Matrona.'

'Matrona.'

'Good. Now quickly, hide. The guards may come in to search for you.'

Peri followed her new mistress to a wardrobe that filled an alcove by the entrance to an inner chamber. She caught a glimpse of hanging silks, scattered cushions and low wooden tables.

'Quickly!' the Matrona urged Peri to step inside the wardrobe where a false back panel had opened. Peri stepped inside through the many hanging dresses that she assumed must belong to the Matrona. A heavy musk perfume still clung to the gowns, making Peri feel that even when the outer wardrobe door was closed the Matrona was still with her. The space between the false panel and the cold wall of rock was cramped. How many other frightened girls had stood here wondering what lay ahead, and what had happened to them? Peri heard muffled voices and decided there was little she could do. The Doctor and his betrayal gnawed at her mind. Why had he called out? Why hazard their lives?

Hidden within the Matrona's chamber Peri felt more isolated and alone than at any other time in her life.

Nine

Yrcanos and the Lukoser had soon put distance between themselves and the chasing guards.

'Wait!' Yrcanos commanded. Obediently the half-man, half-wolf slowed and crouched down on to his haunches. The great shaggy head sank down in misery. 'K ... kill me ...' the jaw and great teeth finally allowed the plea to emerge. With a roar of anger Yrcanos pulled his equerry to his feet and shook him violently. 'You are Dorf of Kanval! Whatever has been done to your body, your spirit must remain intact. Die if you must but achieve that noble end in battle!'

The head of the Wolfman nodded miserably. His yellowed eyes glared at the fur-covered hands he held up before him. Yrcanos saw the fire of revenge glint within the Lukoser's gaze. 'Keep that hatred burning for when you find the man who has done this to you. There is one who betrayed me and a young girl. I have a special death reserved for him.'

'Wh ... who?' the Lukoser asked.

Yrcanos scowled, 'He is a traitor known as the Doctor.'

Serving girls hurried in and out of Kiv's home chamber. Peri waited outside, expecting the Matrona to call her when Lord Kiv demanded his medication. Peri, lightly veiled, as were the other servants, wore a plain smock that she hoped would give her anonymity should Sil or Frax happen to be present.

'Peri . . . !' the Matrona's voice summoned her.

'Matrona?' Peri entered the doorway of the chamber.

'Take this.' The Matrona handed her a bowl with a grey coloured fluid inside. 'You will enter when I call. Not before. Wait outside.'

'I understand, Matrona,' Peri said.

The Matrona returned to the centre of the chamber swirling through the hanging silks. Peri saw green-skinned Mentors in a group around the broad pedestal that supported Lord Kiv. Then the multicoloured swathes of silk drifted back and her view was once again obscured.

Seated near to the Mentors, Crozier watched their leader intently. He recognised the puckers of pain that creased Kiv's mottled face. He noted also the slight slurred speech and the increasingly irrational slips of speech to which the Mentor's leader was becoming prone.

'Aah.' Kiv began to shrink away as if trying to escape from the onset of pain that was building inside his head.

'Matrona!' Crozier called and made an urgent gesture to indicate Kiv's predicament. 'Bring Lord Kiv's ambiotic fluid quickly!'

The Matrona hurried to the door and beckoned Peri to bring the bowl of medication.   Just as Peri was about to enter, the silk pennants disturbed by the Matrona shifted and allowed Peri a view of those seated near to Kiv. With a tingle of shock she saw sitting chatting amicably with Sil, the Doctor.

'I . . . I can't go in . . .' Peri stammered.

'Do you wish me to denounce you?'

Peri shook her head. How stupid, she thought, to be frightened of the Time Lord who had brought her to this benighted planet.

'Obey my order.' The furious tone of the Matrona cut through her thoughts. 'Come, I will go first, there is nothing to fear. Come!'

Perhaps the veil would hide her identity. Peri decided there was no option. She followed in the wake of the Matrona through the hanging silks towards the mentors.

Features twisted by the pain inside his head, the Lord Kiv fumbled for a drinking tube and thrust it into the bowl of fluid held by Peri. The grey liquid diminished rapidly. Kiv did not cease drinking until the bowl was quite empty. Satisfied and with the savage ache already beginning to ease he sank back on to his pedestal.

Peri bowed her head and began to withdraw. Just as she started to relax a voice rang out behind her. The voice of the Doctor.

'You! Bring me another drink. I don't like this, it tastes like swamp water!'

Sil laughed at the Doctor's lack of taste. 'Exactly,' he said.

'Go to them,' the Matrona ordered as she passed Peri on her way to attend to Lord Kiv. There was nothing for it but to obey.

'My Lords,' Peri said, looking down as if abashed by the utter superiority of Sil and the Doctor.

'Bring my friend something better than the water of an inferior swamp. Snail juice, perhaps ...'

Sil laughed with the Doctor joining in. Neither paid any attention to the veiled girl before them. Peri felt like throwing the rejected drinks back at the grinning faces of the loathsome pair but she resisted the impulse and walked to a low serving table where various drinks of vivid hue were lined in rows ready for service.

Across the room Kiv sighed as the medicine brought some relief to his aching head. He looked up at the Matrona gratefully. 'At last the pain eases. Stay near me Matrona – you I trust.'

'The Lord Kiv does me great honour.'

Kiv sighed again. 'Tomorrow I must trust my life to this man of science.'

'What chances of success, my Lord?'

'Equal odds to live or die. I have no choice but to give myself into his hands.'

'Matrona Kani!' Sil's voice shrilled across the chamber. 'See that my Lord Kiv is served only the most wrigglesome of soft sea snakes!'

'I don't need you to tell me that, Sil.'

'No, but I just thought I would!' Sil giggled and the Doctor joined in – two naughty schoolboys ripe for mischief.

Peri filled new glasses with the purple fermented snail's milk that was the champagne of Thoros-Beta and presented the goblets to Sil and the Doctor.

Still chortling, the Doctor sipped his drink. The sour taste offended his palate. 'What is in this drink?' he snapped at the girl.

'Everyone else is drinking it, I thought ...'

The face of the Doctor contorted with rage, 'You *thought*, who are you to ...'

Peri couldn't bear the sight of him. 'Oh, shut up, Doctor!'

'How does the servitor know the name of the Doctor?' Kiv asked.

'Because, my Lord ...' the Doctor said softly. 'She is a spy!'

73

With a sudden movement he whisked away the flimsy veil from Peri's face.

'This,' the Doctor continued in a gloating voice, 'is the girl who ran from the Induction Centre. She no doubt intended to poison every one of us in due course.'

'What?' Kiv reacted with alarm.

'I prepared your medication myself,' the Matrona calmed the agitation of the Mentor.

'Doctor, please ...' Peri began.

Sil decided a decisive show of authority would impress his master. 'She must confess. Guards ... take her to the Rock of Sorrows!'

With a guard holding each arm, Peri began to be dragged out of the chamber. 'Doctor, please help me!' she called back plaintively. But the Doctor remained impervious to the appeals of the girl and on the Matrix his face, in close-up, seemed impassive and uncaring.

'That's the ploy. I remember now!'

The Doctor was on his feet. Trembling with relief and excitement.

'Ploy, Doctor?' said the Valeyard not bothering even to rise from his seat.

'Yes, yes, my plan to remove us both from the heart of the Mentors' domain. I gambled that after I'd helped Crozier fix their celebral transference unit, they might just trust me to interrogate Peri alone.'

'To what end?' the Valeyard drawled the question out innocently.

'Escape, I should imagine,' said the Doctor, the certainty of the purity of his motives lessening through the attitude of confidence displayed by the Valeyard.

'Did the interrogation take place?' the Inquisitor asked.

'It certainly did, Sagacity.' Again that worrying smile played about the cruel mouth of the prosecuting counsel.

'I would wish to see that.'

As soon as the words had passed from the Inquisitor's lips, Zon activated the Matrix recall systems and the scene changed to a view of a pillar of rock on the shoreline of the Sea of Sorrows. Above the skyline, low in the sky, hung the twin planet of Thoros-Alpha. The aspect changed and a much closer view of the perpendicular rock could be seen with the incoming tide beginning to lap against the base of the rock. Again the Matrix focus changed – this time to a different angle with the pillar seen from the shore.

Chained to the rock, Peri was reacting with panic as the pink sea foam started to wash over her shoes.

Opposite the Rock of Sorrows lay a cave whose entrance was surrounded by tangled mauve vegetation. From this cave came a figure in a red coat who picked his way carefully over the rugged shore towards Peri.

'What do you want?' Peri's voice was tossed towards him but the sound of the incoming sea took away any tone of defiance it might have carried.

The Doctor reached his erstwhile companion. He regarded her for a long time without speaking. Then he gripped her arm, hard.

'Ow!'

'Mentor Sil fears conspiracy against the Lord Kiv. You are a spy for the Alphan terrorists!' Slowly the grip of the Doctor exerted pressure on her inner arm.

'What? Ow, stop that!'

The Doctor put his lips next to Peri's left ear. 'We can speak now,' he whispered. 'No one can hear.'

Relief lifted Peri's spirits. 'Oh, Doctor, I thought that

transference pulse had made you crazy.'

'I'm your friend, you know that.'

'I began to wonder.'

'I only want to help you, Peri.'

The Doctor's voice seemed smooth and sincere. Peri looked down at the sea now swirling round her knees and tugged at the chains. 'How do I get out of here?'

'Easy.' The Doctor stepped away from an incoming wave.

'How?' Peri asked eagerly.

'By simply telling me who are the Alphans leading the unrest and how we can annihilate them!'

The Doctor's words sent Peri's heart tumbling down into despair. 'What?' her voice faltered. 'Alphans ... I don't...'

The face of the Doctor was seized by a terrible rage. 'Answer me! Can you not feel the tide rising all around you. Unless you wish to add your despair to all those who have perished in the Sea of Sorrows I suggest you tell me everything!'

In the Tidal Control chamber, Sil, Kiv and Crozier watched Peri and the Doctor on a monitor screen. As the Doctor's last words brought terror to Peri, Sil cackled, 'Just like the old days. There is nothing more enjoyable than watching other people suffer!'

The mad giggle was only stemmed by Sil passing a Marsh Minnow from a nearby plate to his mouth. Crozier watched the green creature wriggle on Sil's dark tongue and then turned away in disgust.

'Confess!' the Doctor demanded.

'To what?' Peri yelled at him, the water now around her waist.

'Your guilt, your bungling. Your Alphan friends, everything, you must help the Mentors; you must help me!'

'Doctor, what's happened to you?'

'I see my own interest, I place myself first!'

'What about me?'

The expression of the Doctor became even more malevolent. 'You are expendable. You have no value. Tomorrow they plan to take the brain of Kiv and transfer it into my skull. He will possess my body. I will be no more. To prevent that I *must* please the Mentors, and if that means you must be sacrificed in my place that is how it must be!'

Then the Doctor raised his fist.

'Tell me everything you know!'

Peri tried to cower away from the blow that was coming. She looked into the eyes of the Doctor and saw only manic rage. She braced herself to receive blows from the Time Lord she had once admired and loved.

Ten

'Enough!' Crozier's voice crackled from a voice relay unit hidden in the mouth of the cave.

Just about to launch a savage attack the Doctor hesitated then called back, 'I won't kill her. Just a little assault and battery to help her memory.'

'You will not damage her. This exercise was as much to test you as her. Release the girl, Doctor, at once!'

Sullenly, the Doctor did as he was ordered. Taking out of his pocket a small key, he waded out into the water to unlock the metal clasp that held the chains.

Peri, feeling the links loosen and fall from her, tried to dash away but the tide hampered her efforts and allowed the greater strength of the Doctor to wade at a faster rate through the sea. He soon caught up with Peri and subdued her by twisting an arm behind her back. This accomplished, he began to march the wet and miserable girl towards the mouth of the cave.

In court, the Doctor jumped to his feet.

'It was never like that!'

'How can you be certain?' the Valeyard rose quickly to the challenge. 'You have no clear memory of the incident and the Matrix never lies.'

'I wonder,' the Doctor muttered.

The Inquisitor interrupted. 'May we continue? I grow tired of these constant interruptions.'

'I am at your disposal, Sagacity.'

The Valeyard bowed. His black gown hanging to the floor, made him look like a giant crow reaching to pull a worm up from the ground.

'It was never like that!' the Doctor yelled again. Even to his ears his cry seemed desperate; blustering; hysterical.

The Inquisitor took the same view. 'Enough, Doctor! The Matrix does not lie, cannot lie. You are aware of that fact. Why persist in contradictory statements?'

The Doctor felt that all was lost. He could feel the jury of Time Lords staring curiously at him. They revealed the fascination that all juries are supposed to show for the demeanour of a person they have decided is guilty.

The Doctor opened his mouth to speak but no words would come. There was nothing for him to do but return abjectly to his seat.

'Proceed!' the Inquisitor instructed.

Stealthily King Yrcanos and his Equerry, the Wolfman, Dorf, had made their way back towards the heart of the Mentors' underground complex. Once they had outrun the guards they had circled around the maze of tunnels and now found themselves entering a passageway that seemed occupied by a series of small cells barred from ceiling to floor.

They were about to explore further when the Lukoser whined a warning that sent them both into hiding. They watched as towards them came the Doctor, Peri and two guards, one of whom began to unlock a cell.

'The Doctor,' Yrcanos breathed.

'Do we attack?' the Lukoser asked.

'Of course. That dreg is my enemy. Let us advance.'
Baring his teeth the Lukoser began to pad along the
passage with Yrcanos close behind. Oblivious to the
danger bearing down upon him, the Doctor started to
push Peri into the cell.

'What's happened to you, Doctor? Why do you hate
me so?' Peri really wanted to understand. She scanned
the Doctor's set expression of cold hostility.

'I must do what I think is best,' was the flat reply.

Peri felt the tears within her. 'I thought you were
different, that you cared for justice, truth, good.' Her
eyes began to fill with tears. 'Oh, go away; I can't bear to
look at what you are now!'

'Peri...' the Doctor started to speak but was
interrupted by a ferocious war cry.

'Sohraantaap!'

With the impact of surprise Yrcanos and the Lukoser
wreaked havoc on the group. Although the guards put up
some initial resistance they were soon overcome.
Holding out a phaser weapon taken from one of the
guards Yrcanos aimed after the Doctor, who, at the first
inkling of who the attackers were, had run away with
great alacrity.

Just as he was about to squeeze the activation panel,
the weapon was swept from the hand of the King.

Angrily Yrcanos turned on the saviour of the Doctor.
It was Peri.

'What have you done, my lady? Because of you that
vermin still lives!'

'I... I couldn't help it.' Peri's voice faltered. 'The
Doctor – what you say about him is true, but he wasn't
always like that.'

'We had better leave here...' Yrcanos said grumpily.
'The Doctor will no doubt alert our enemies as soon as he

can.'

'Yes,' Peri agreed dolefully and tagged along with the Lukoser and his master who strode ahead, occasionally turning a puzzled look back at a girl foolish enough to spare someone who was so obviously her enemy.

'Toady! Coward! Turncoat!'

The Valeyard lashed the Doctor with the words. All the Doctor could do was shake his head in dumb denial.

'You were afraid that Crozier wanted to transplant the brain of Kiv into your head. You said as much yourself. That thought, Doctor, sent you into a blind panic!'

'I've told you – it was a ploy. I . . . I wouldn't want to harm Peri, would I?'

'You have no clear memory of events on Thoros-Beta, have you?'

'I can recall some of it. Bits are beginning to bob back into my mind.'

'Oh, really? And does any of your convenient and sudden recall agree with anything that the court has already seen?'

'No . . . I mean . . . yes . . . but the emphasis is wrong.'

'What does that mean, Doctor?'

'The events took place but not quite as we've just seen them.' The Doctor frowned perplexedly. It did not make sense what he seemed to be saying. What was he saying? What had happened to his sense of recall?

The Inquisitor decided to break the lengthening silence in which the Doctor was marooned. 'Doctor, it occurs to me that your current mental condition makes it very difficult for you to defend yourself. I would therefore suggest that this court be adjourned.'

'No!' the Doctor protested. 'I want this trial to continue.'

'Then might I suggest you engage a court defender . . .'

'No!' the Doctor said in a voice so determined that the Inquisitor did not pursue the matter further but noted on a pad before her that the proposal had been made but that the accused had rejected the offer of proper representation.

The Valeyard smiled thinly as he addressed the Inquisitor. 'Might I suggest that we go no further into the distressing aspects of the Doctor's guilt. I suggest you give your judgement now. I submit that the Doctor forfeit this and all his future lives in retribution for his crimes on Thoros-Beta.'

The Inquisitor considered the Valeyard's request for some time. Then reached a decision. 'Request denied. You have not yet furnished the court with sufficient evidence. Proceed!'

'That is to become my new body?' Kiv looked down into what could have been a coffin. Laid out inside the rectangular box was a near replica of himself.

Crozier joined Kiv in looking down at the donor. 'The coastguards found him adrift among the Isles of Brak. He is of the same branch of mutation, almost certainly from your home mire, my Lord.'

'He does look like a younger me.'

'Not quite so handsome, Magnificence.'

Sil had joined them. 'Be quiet, Sil.' Kiv could feel the onset of another crushing attack of pain while Crozier was pointing at the tip of the donor body.

'He has retained the primeval sting. His tail contains venom enough to kill.'

'Fascinating.' Kiv frowned as a stab of torment struck at the base of his skull. 'I could perhaps sting all my incompetent assistants to death.'

Crozier and Sil exchanged uneasy looks. 'Are you certain the new skull will be large enough, Crozier?' Sil asked. His voice was anxious and trembling.

'The capacity is only a little larger in volume than that of the Lord Kiv. The operation will give us a little more time to find a permanent host.'

The door to the laboratory opened. The Doctor entered with a guard who had guided him back to the centre for experiment and investigation.

Sil turned to the Doctor, his gaze flickering over the size of the visitor's head speculatively. 'We must make every effort to find the right head on the correct body.'

'I have some possibilities to explore. Have you come to assist me in the consciousness transfer, Doctor?' asked Crozier.

'Yes, thought I might.'

'You can monitor the BTV.'

'I would be pleased to.'

Kiv suddenly could remain stoical under the pressure of his expanding brain crushing against the unremitting structure of his skull. 'Let us begin!'

'Yes, my Lord.' Crozier helped Kiv on to the operating table. Kiv lay back and squinted up into the glare of the white lights above. He wondered if this painful light would be the last thing he would ever see. He felt the sting of a needle. A drowsiness began to creep over him. Summoning enough energy he managed to jerk out a final threat, 'Should this transfer not work and brain death occur, my bearers have orders ... orders to liquify all who failed to ... save ... my ... life ...'

Crozier took his hands from the decontamination box. He glanced around at the agglomeration of technology linked to the cerebral transference units all buzzing and glowing in readiness for the most challenging operation of his life. He watched the Matrona place the donor body on another table alongside the now unconscious Kiv.

'I am ready,' Crozier said calmly.

The Matrona came to his side, carrying a box of surgical instruments. 'Check antilymphocyte drip,' she ordered.

'Checked,' the Doctor answered. 'Active.'

'Laser scalpel.' Crozier felt the instrument slap into his hand. There was no option left. Out of the side of his eye Crozier could see the guards with their phaser weapons poised to punish any slip, any failure. Then the scientist blanked everything from his mind except the intricate task in hand. He made an incision at the base of Kiv's skull and as the spurt of green blood stained the white surface of the table he guided the helmet of the brain transference support system across to hover over the two fawn-coloured reptilian bodies.

'Where exactly are we going?' Peri was tired of marching behind Yrcanos.

The King halted his purposeful stride. 'As with all corrupt dictatorships, there are bound to be pockets of resistance working and plotting to overthrow the Mentor class.'

'Suppose there is such a group, what good would that do us?'

'My belief is that all they await is a great leader.'

'Like who?' asked Peri.

'Like me. I am he.'

Peri was not quite certain how to take the boast. 'I'm sure you would be very effective. But do these resistance fighters know that?'

'They will learn.'

'Maybe they'd prefer to remain ignorant, worse still

they might see our interference as a threat and kill us. I've got a better idea. Let's get back to the TARDIS.' Peri began to move off.

'Wait!' Yrcanos bellowed after her. Peri halted in her tracks.

'These resistance fighters will only be Alphans. They will need leadership if they are ever to triumph.'

'Mm ... my great King is right ...' the Lukoser spoke haltingly.

'But how will he find these people?' Peri said, her voice filled with doubt.

'They will find us. I sense it.'

Yrcanos looked so determined, so convinced of his destiny, that Peri weakened a little. 'All right but let's rest first, then march.' She smiled at the King, gave his bush of a beard a gentle tug. 'There's a good Warlord.'

The Lukoser whined agreement and squatted with his back to the wall. Peri joined him, splaying her tired legs out in front of her.

'Agreed,' said Yrcanos, reluctantly, 'but only for a moment ...' Then he joined his army of two in resting against the wall of the rock. The Lukoser whined mournfully.

'He sounds hungry,' said Peri.

'I'm not surprised, so am I, Yrcanos, famished.'

The Warlord reached into a pouch hanging from his broad studded belt. 'Here ...' Peri took what looked like a strip of dried wood. 'Go on, try it, eat, my lady ...'

With some trepidation the girl put the morsel into her mouth and closed her teeth on to it. The taste was wild and startlingly strong. *Too* strong. 'Ugh!' She spat out the strip of dried provision. Before the food had reached the floor the Lukoser had caught and swallowed the scrap of food.

'What was that!' Peri choked, still recovering from the shock to her palate.

Yrcanos pulled out a strip for himself and began chewing on the piece with much relish. 'Flay fish, it sustains your body, fuels your fighting spirit.'

'But doesn't delight your taste buds.'

'What are they?'

'Never mind.'

While Yrcanos continued to chew, the Lukoser stretched out alongside Peri and with his head on his paws went into an immediate sleep. Without thinking Peri scratched between his fur-covered shoulders. In his sleep the Lukoser began to whimper pitiously.

'Stop it!' Yrcanos pulled Peri away from stroking the Lukoser. 'Dorf is, or was, a warrior. He has no use for gentleness and pity.'

'Oh, no?' said Peri as the drowsing animal nudged up to her.

'Huh... he... je... jealous,' the Lukoser said sleepily.

'I am not!' Yrcanos jumped to his feet, raised a foot ready to aim a kick at the ribs of the man-wolf.

'C'mon boys! What's the matter with you two? We've enough guys against us without you two needing to kick lumps out of each other!'

The words of the girl prevented a clash but King and Equerry continued to glower at each other. Then Yrcanos laughed. 'You are quite right, it is the flay fish. My fault. It makes one want to do battle, I should have saved it for our next skirmish.'

'Good.' Peri started to relax, which was a mistake, for Yrcanos was already stamping up and down, his mind feverish with plans for fierce encounters.

'We must move, my lady, locate our allies and prepare

to do battle unto death!'

One thing at a time, huh?' Peri tried to slow him down. 'Let's see if we can find this so called Alphan resistance and let them know we're on their side.'

'Yes,' was all the King said before he marched away.

Peri and the Lukoser began to follow. They felt like a very meagre army but the King seemed to have little fear of achieving his ambition of freeing all the slaves who had fallen in thrall to the Mentors.

Eleven

'Donor brain in position,' Crozier made a final adjustment above the body that would soon, if all went well, play host to the brain of Lord Kiv.

'EEE readings in recipient conjunction.'

'Thank you, Doctor.'

'Why is this taking so long?' Sil's voice interrupted.

'Go for a walk, Sil, you're like an anxious parent,' the Doctor said, his eyes never leaving the neural readings on which all their lives depended.

Sil pointed a stubby finger at the open brain of Kiv. 'The wealth of the whole planet depends on that lump of green tissue there ... I haven't learned all his secrets yet...'

Crozier became aware of someone talking needlessly. His pale eyes darted to Sil. 'Stop gyrating your throat. I'm about to attempt reactivation of brain tissue.'

Sil looked upwards into the lights set in the ceiling of the laboratory and began to babble. 'Please, Great Morgo, let them succeed!'

Crozier was oblivious once more to everything but the brain transference operation. 'Doctor, prepare for independent support mode. The reading should reach twenty-one point five six.'

'Twenty-one point five six.'

Carefully the Matrona brought up the impulse balance between Kiv and the donor. She called out, 'Approaching twenty dead...'

'Don't say dead...' Sil groaned, unable to look now that the critical point was approaching. Surreptitiously he indicated that his bearers should move towards the door. They were well bribed to make a dash for freedom with him should the worst happen. Could he trust them? Sil was not sure. He regretted the bullying and abuse he had heaped on them in the past.

'Morgo, let Lord Kiv live and I will sacrifice seven Alphan rejects in thanks.' Sil breathed his fervent prayer and closed his eyes in trepidation as the critical phase of the transplant approached.

'Twenty-one ... three ... five-*six*!' Simultaneously the Doctor and the Matrona levelled their input power balancing the electronic line that should have registered heartbeat on Kiv's screen. The link remained incomplete; of respiratory function there was none.

'There's nothing, no heart, no brain readings, nothing! We have failed...' The Matrona began to panic.

The guns of the guards came up.

Sil began to gabble. 'They joke, bad taste, a profitless humourless quip... tell them, Crozier!'

Crozier looked drained of all emotion. Sil turned to his unmoving bearers. 'Half my fortune... five minutes start...'

'Look!' the Doctor pointed at Kiv's chest. 'His chest gills lifted. Matrona, did the oxygen unit register its input?'

The Matrona tested a switch. 'Nothing.'

'Reserve quickly...' Crozier ordered, hope returning frantic energy to his actions.

'Switch to the endoradiotine, Doctor!'

The Doctor did as Crozier suggested. Still no sign of further life from Kiv in his new body. The Mentor stretched out, lifeless, on the table unmoving except for a slight drawing of breath. The shell of his former being lay dead on the table nearby.

The Doctor decided to gamble and boosted the antilymphocyte drip tenfold. The effect was as startling as it was dramatic. The readings of neural activity waves streamed across the screen in long curving lines that soon settled into a steady looping wave. On another unit, the heartline on the cardiograph pinged strongly. Kiv stirred. Sil clapped his hands madly, the guards lowered their guns.

'Strange witless humour... like I said,' Sil said, weakly.

'Thanks for your moral support, Sil,' Crozier said, bitingly.

'Yes,' the Doctor added, 'nice to know you can always be relied on to be your usual treacherous self.'

Sil smiled. He cared only about one thing – he was alive. 'I endeavour to maintain a certain continuity of behaviour just like you, Doctor. Now attend to the Lord Kiv, see that he stays alive in his beautiful new body!'

Peri thought something was different about the corridor they now found themselves trudging down. Smell? No... though there seemed less tang of the sea. Less vapour. Sound? There was no sound apart from the clump of Yrcanos and the pad-pad of the Lukoser. What then? Peri could not decide but there was certainly something different. Behind her, a panel slid open in the rough hewn wall. An Alphan, dressed in tan poncho and yellow and red headband of a tribal chieftain, stepped out and waved to his companions to join him. Soon a small group began shadowing the trio ahead.

'Stop!' Yrcanos ordered. He had noticed an opening appearing in the tunnel well ahead. A young Alphan male, almost as imposing in stature as Yrcanos, stepped out of the wall ahead to confront them. Yrcanos turned, saw that they were between two forces and smiled at Peri.

'I told you they would find us. Now to convince them of my right to lead them.'

The Warlord thumped himself on his breastplate. 'I am King Yrcanos!'

The bulky Alphan seemed unimpressed.

'Hold your tongue.'

'I...' Yrcanos started. Tuza, the leader of the Alphans arrived and indicated the dark side passageway in the tunnel wall.

'This way... unless you wish to die here.'

'OK. Love to,' Peri said wishing to head off a battle royal between Yrcanos and the Alphans. She ducked into the entrance that led off the main passage and found herself in a natural gallery.

Peri walked along a natural causeway that crossed a lake of pink brackish water and disappeared into a series of caves carved out of limestone. The honeycomb of caves were crumbling but seemed, after the gloomy interiors of the section they had just left, to be beautiful in their disparate shapes. Peri pointed out strange formations carved out by the tides over millions of years. The Lukoser moved his head up and down as if he understood. Maybe it was the change of scene but Peri began to feel a little more cheerful. Tuza and his henchmen stayed close behind, watching every move the trio made. Peri had no way of knowing that they were being led towards a terrifying ordeal.

In the laboratory an elated Crozier finished his examination of the donor body that now showed all signs of renewed life. 'Success, Doctor, after a decade of work, I can transform the evolutionary process, conquer death – the possibilities are endless!'

'Are you sure? Aren't you concerned about tissue rejection?' The Doctor was doubtful.

'I have perfected a plasma serum to prevent just that. From today, Doctor, thanks to your help, I can put any brain into any body anywhere!'

Sil interrupted the discussion. 'Now that you have assisted in a miracle of science perhaps you would consent to help me achieve a similar feat of commerce?'

The Doctor glanced at Crozier. 'How long will it be before Kiv might regain consciousness?'

'One hour, two . . .'

'I am at your service, Sil.' The Doctor bowed to the mentor.

Yrcanos, the Lukoser and Peri were splayed out on the ground and tightly bound. All they could see was the roof of a natural gallery. Into their view came a burly Alphan. They watched as the Alphan looked about for a suitably large stone to drop down on to their heads.

'So much for your charisma,' Peri said to Yrcanos. Her voice was full of fear at their predicament. 'Tell them again. Tell them we are on their side. Please.'

'Me – a King, beg to that rabble?'

The Lukoser growled as Tuza came to look down upon them. The Alphan leader raised an arm to the man on the rock above who held a small boulder and was preparing to smash it down upon them.

Peri twisted her head to look at Yrcanos. He was staring stoically up at the sight of his imminent death.

Tuza began to speak with a slight trace of regret. 'You must understand that we cannot allow your bodies and skulls to be retrieved undamaged so that brain surgery can be performed to create creatures like this.' His foot indicated the Lukoser.

'Wait!' Peri interrupted. 'We're like you. We're against brain alteration. The Lukoser does not wish to be as he is. He was made like that by the Mentors! I was a captive of the Mentors too. King Yrcanos is a hostage, valuable to them only so they can exploit his people. Please do not destroy us unless you wish to please the Mentors!'

'The Mentors.' Tuza's face twisted into hatred.

Yrcanos spoke calmly. 'She speaks truth. I do not beg. Pulverise my skull and you slay an ally. But supply me with weapons and a good band of fighting men, and I will bring triumph against our mutual enemies.'

Tuza thought about the words for a long moment, then made a motion with his hand to the Alphan above. The burly executioner lowered the boulder to his feet and Peri breathed once more.

Tuza bent down to them. 'I have heard of King Yrcanos. I had to prove that you were really he. You will have a plan, your Majesty?'

'Untie me and you will hear it!'

'Crozier!' The Matrona's voice was wild with panic as she bent over the body that now belonged to Lord Kiv. 'Something's wrong!'

Crozier checked every reading available. 'But he was fine a moment ago. He's suffering cardiac arrest. His body is reacting against the drugs.' Panic-stricken, Crozier began to massage Kiv's chest, trying to stimulate the leader's flagging heartbeat.

'Don't die on me...' he pleaded. The Matrona watched Crozier pound Kiv's chest, knowing that not only the Mentor's life was threatened by that faltering heartbeat.

Unaware of the developing crisis in the laboratory Sil was seated in Kiv's chair showing off his prowess as controller of the Profit Room technology.

'Look, Doctor, money, money! All the stock and commodity markets are available to us via warpfold relay – see there...'

Sil pointed to a display screen that filled a complete wall. 'There is an application for credit.' Sil paused and punched a keyboard before him. On the screen appeared further details of the request – 'Search-conv Corp', identifying the application for credit.

'Who are they?' the Doctor asked.

Sil snorted derisively. 'They're nothing much. A bunch of burnt-out space rangers who search for wrecked space ships. They request funding to purchase another retrieval craft, which I will deny.' Sil reached for the reject button.

'Wait...' The Doctor frowned in an effort of recall or perhaps it should have been described as precall for the events were from a little time ahead in the future. 'Planet of Tokl, 24th century. I think there are to be many space battles around the Rim Worlds at that time. There'll probably be a heap of battle-cruiser debris floating out there soon.'

'For this company to retrieve?'

'If they have the equipment to do it.'

Sil giggled with delight. 'How useful to have a Time Lord in one's employ... I will allow their application for credit.'

He pressed the 'Credit agreed' button and leaned back as if he had completed a week's work. A servant brought Sil his favourite snack. The green wigglesome delicacies writhed on the platter. Sil offered the dish to his guest.

'Marsh Minnow, Doctor?'

Absently the Doctor helped himself and popped a minnow into his mouth. A taste like a mixture of iron filings mixed with used engine oil blighted the taste buds of the Time Lord. 'Ugh!' He spat out the offending minnow.

Sil grinned while gobbling down his lunch greedily. 'I should have warned you Doctor, they are something of an acquired taste.'

'I can believe it,' gasped the Doctor shuddering at the memory of the experience.

Sil gobbled down the last titbit and sighed contentedly. 'The Lord Kiv will be most pleased with me for my great foresight over those space rangers. I must be sure that I am the first familiar face he sees with his new eyes.'

'That would be comforting for him ... should we go and see how the patient is getting on?'

The Doctor sat in the courtroom and despaired at the sight of himself consorting with his enemy, Sil.

He lifted his head and spoke quietly. 'My actions cannot be as they seem.'

The Valeyard was quickly on the attack. 'Perhaps you would tell us why a Time Lord with all his privileges should not only meddle in a swamp world like Thoros-Beta but also help the Mentors make money from his inside knowledge of the future.'

'There is an explanation, there must be ... yet I can't recall it. There has to be some event my mind won't let me recall.' The Doctor stood up, fists clenched, and stared wildly around the court.

'Are you unwell?' the Inquisitor asked. 'Perhaps you would like me to call for a recess, Doctor?'

'No!' the Doctor's voice was fierce with a determination not heard before. 'I've had enough of wondering why I acted as I did on Thoros-Beta. Let's get to it. Let's find out what happened. Play the Matrix, let it show what it will!'

Twelve

'How is the Lord Kiv?' Sil enquired as he entered the lab with the Doctor. The Matrona and Crozier glanced at each other.

'He has had a crisis ...' the Matrona began.

'Crisis. Crisis ... what ... what?' Sil said with alarm.

'He's through it now,' Crozier said.

'When will he wake up?' Sil asked, staring at his master who lay, unmoving, eyes closed, on the operating table.

'Soon. Soon,' the Matrona said soothingly.

'There has been some cardiac flutter. A little worrying neural activity, some piczoelectric imaging array.'

'That's all right, then,' said Sil. 'I will stay here and await Kiv's return to life. Sit down, Doctor, you may wait too.'

To pass the time the Doctor began to check the equipment that clustered all around the unconscious Thoros-Betan leader. He was thinking that Kiv should have returned to consciousness by now if what Crozier had boasted about had really been achieved and a living brain been transposed from one head to another.

Yrcanos had expounded his plan to Tuza and the other Alphans. They were impressed by Yrcanos and his belief in ultimate victory but Tuza had a remaining doubt.

'Your aim is a sound one, but our men are untrained.'

'Under my leadership, they will fight like demons!'

Peri tried to interject a note of sanity. 'Yrcanos, let's not get too carried away, I know it's nice to have a few guys to command.'

The Lukoser opened his great jaws. 'I have se...see...seen him inspire disheartened rabble to acts of he...heroism.'

'But how many survived?' Peri said gloomily.

Yrcanos moved an impatient step. 'A minor consideration when glory is to be won.'

Tuza interrupted the growing dissension. 'We do not have anything to lose. At present all we do is hide like vermin. King Yrcanos of the Krontep, we will follow you!'

'But will you fight?'

'Yes!' The Alphans followed Tuza's lead.

'Vroomnik!' Yrcanos yelled. His shout exultant and booming over too far a distance for Peri's liking. 'Now to your weapon dump and on to glory!'

'Here we go again,' said Peri as Yrcanos went striding off with even more purpose than ever. After six strides he turned and raised his right arm. His new followers paused expectantly. 'This hand that has not touched steel for what seems an age, I dedicate to the service of gaining your liberty!'

The Alphans cheered. Tuza spoke quietly to Ger, a trusted confidant. 'Find Sorn and his men. Tell him the day of action has finally come.' Ger nodded and left the group, while Yrcanos and Tuza became engrossed in a discussion of tactics and resources.

'Look!' Peri called out, drawing their attention to an old man tottering towards them. Peri ran to support the white-haired Alphan who stumbled and fell before she could reach him.

'What's happened. What can we do to help?'

The old man tried to raise himself but his failing strength caused him to collapse on his side and Peri could see his life-force draining away. Soon the struggle was over.

'What happened?' Peri asked bewilderedly.

'Old age.' Yrcanos shrugged.

'Wait...' Tuza pushed between them and knelt alongside the dead man. 'Linna. Is it Linna?'

'You knew him?' Yrcanos asked.

Tuza did not reply but stared down at the wizened face in disbelief.

'He was a spice trader back home on Thoros-Alpha. I can't believe what I see.'

Yrcanos could not understand the fuss.

'Death comes to us all. He has lived a long life.'

'Linna was no older than I am. Twenty years old, not a hundred. How has he turned into an old man?'

'Maybe through this...' Peri pointed at a patch of blood on the base of the dead man's skull. A small dart protruded from the wrinkled skin of the deceased.

'Don't touch,' Peri warned Tuza. 'That could be responsible for his rapid ageing!'

'This is the work of the Mentors!'

Tuza clenched his fists in helpless rage.

'What was the dead warrior's function?'

'He was one of the guardians of our weapons store.'

'I smell trickery, betrayal!' Yrcanos scowled fiercely and glared in the direction from which Linna had appeared.

'I'll scout ahead,' Tuza said and started to move away.

Yrcanos grabbed the leader of the Alphans. 'We'll all

scout ahead.'

'No. There could be much danger.'

'Good. Then we will advance on it together!'

The small group began to advance towards whatever was waiting ahead. Peri, marching along with them, could not keep from her mind the thought that they were involved in a futile mission against forces who possessed an arsenal of frightening weapons. Peri held out her hand. It was brown, shapely and young. She imagined it wrinkled, spotted, old. A fur-covered paw appeared and stroked her hand comfortingly.

'Thanks,' said Peri grateful for the touch and the Lukoser's presence beside her. He was a walking testament to the Mentor's ruthless regime. Peri decided that she had no choice but to support Yrcanos in his ambition to overthrow the evil rulers of Thoros-Beta.

'Why has Lord Kiv not yet returned to life?'

'It takes time,' the Doctor said.

'You are allowing the Lord Kiv to die!'

Alerted by the shrill panic of Sil the guards moved in, phasers ready to liquify Crozier and his helpers.

'Wait.' Crozier held up a hand. 'Doctor, the severin drip.'

The Doctor knew this was Crozier's last throw. The dial showed five. The Doctor adjusted the flow of the adrenalin-based stimulant.

'A movement!' the Matrona called from beside Kiv.

'A reaction here,' the Doctor confirmed a strengthening neural wave on the Personascan.

Crozier saw Kiv's eyelids flutter open then close. 'It's going to work!' he said exultantly.

Sil bounced up and down on his carrying frame. 'Lift me, lift me! My face must be the first civilised thing he sees!'

The bearers obeyed their master and raised Sil so that he could look down on Kiv.

The eyes of the patient opened. He saw a world of distorted images, blurred colours. Yellow, red, blue. Then a slow focus began that became first a large blob of green, then Kiv's eyes saw a leering face, his ears heard a grating voice. 'My Lord,' it said. 'Welcome back.'

Kiv screamed. 'Have I died and gone into the belly of Sanscrupa?'

'Magnificence, it's me – Sil.'

Kiv began to weep.

'Why do you cry, my Lord?'

'I dreamed I was lost in the Sea of Longing.'

Crozier intervened. 'Dreams were to be expected. Side effects of the sedation. Nothing to worry about.'

'I feel only a little different. An ache in my ... I suppose I can say my skull.'

Crozier smiled, elated with the success of his coup. 'That will be your skull until we can find one that will be a permanent home for your intellect.'

'The Great Morgo be praised ...' Sil began to intone.

Kiv shut him off by attempting to rise. 'I must to work. There is a future commodity deadline for the Sondlex crop on Wilson One.'

'It will be attended to,' Sil smirked. 'The Doctor and I have struck up a profitable partnership.'

'Oh?' The yellow eyes looked with suspicion from one to the other. 'Nothing ... not speculation, I trust.'

The Doctor bowed to the new body that now contained the brain and spirit of the financial genius. 'Merely conserving resources until you return to your rightful place as Supreme Master of us all.'

*

Crossing a small cavern Yrcanos, Peri and Tuza approached a rockfall that seemed to block the tunnel completely. Yrcanos noted the crevices and alcoves that ran in both directions from either side of the obstacle.

'My other men have yet to arrive,' Tuza said.

'No matter. Where are the weapons?' Yrcanos asked.

'Behind there.'

'Where?'

'Someone has blocked the entrance with a fall of rocks.'

'Or an accident,' Peri said.

Tuza shook his head. 'If so, it's a very convenient rock slip. It covers the only entrance to our weapons store.'

The Lukoser and the Alphans arrived.

'Wh ... what's happened?' the Lukoser asked.

Yrcanos pointed. 'Our enemies may have brought the rocks down. A woman's way of fighting.'

'Thanks a lot,' Peri said.

'If these Mentors were anything but cowards they would show their banners and fight in the open!'

'Let's get away from here,' Peri suggested. 'Wait for the other Alphan guys to turn up.'

'She has a point,' Tuza said.

Yrcanos pounded his breastplate. 'I am Yrcanos, King of ...'

'We've heard all that!' Peri yelled with sudden exasperation. 'Whereas it terrifies me, I'm not certain it will have the same effect on whoever caused that fall of rock.'

The Lukoser began to speak. 'There is vic ... victory to be had, great King but let it be in pru ... prudence this day.'

'You are a great dog of war ... I mean ...' Yrcanos corrected himself. 'A great soldier ... whose advice I trust and value. So, for today, prudence will be our watchword. Tomorrow, however, I shall soak the land in blood.'

Peri relaxed. 'I'm glad we've got that sorted out.'

Yrcanos smiled condescendingly down upon her. His hand reached and touched under her chin. 'Let us withdraw, my lady. You and I will find a pleasing way to spend the time before the rest of Tuza's warriors arrive.'

'It would please me if you weren't so patronising . . .' A shift in the jumble of rock interrupted Peri. 'What's happening . . . ?'

'Look!' Tuza pointed to where an arm had appeared between two boulders.

Quickly Tuza darted to the rockfall and began heaving and scrabbling at the tumble of boulders, trying to free the body whose arm had appeared. Yrcanos and the Alphans also ran to assist in the clearance.

Peri was about to join them when the Lukoser caught her arm. 'Wait, there could be da . . . da . . . danger.'

Cautiously they looked about them, the Lukoser sniffing the air. Nothing seemed amiss. If they were being watched, their enemies were well hidden. Peri and the man-wolf joined the group at the rocks in time to see an ancient lined face revealed.

'Ger, it is Ger!' Sure enough, when they all looked closely the young Alphan sent to assemble the supporting rebels was now a husk of an old man crushed beneath the weight of the rocks.

'No!' Tuza tried to pull his friend from the burial pile.

'Leave him!' Yrcanos reached to restrain Tuza.

'Do not move, anyone!' a sharp voice ordered from behind the group. Frax appeared on a ledge above them. Below his guards appeared, armed with phaser weapons.

'Stand still and you live. Resist . . .'

The threat did not need to be completed. The Alphan group was surrounded completely.

'That isn't my fault!' In the courtroom of Galifrey the Doctor could stand no more of what the Matrix was inexorably showing of his time on Thoros-Beta.

'You can't blame me for that ...' his finger jabbed towards the screen that was frozen into stillness with the Alphans, Yrcanos, Peri and the Lukoser at the mercy of Frax and his heavily armed guards. 'I wasn't even at the weapons store!'

'All that has taken place you are indirectly responsible for,' the Valeyard said, firmly.

'No! Please, my lady ...' the Doctor pleaded to the Inquisitor. 'The death of Ger and the other freedom fighters wasn't my fault!'

'Your presence on that planet did influence events. There isn't any way that can be denied.'

The Doctor sat down. He put his head in his hands.

'Doctor,' the Valeyard's mocking voice drifted lazily across the courtroom. 'Look at the screen, Doctor, don't miss the tragic results of your folly!'

The screen activated with the Mentor guards dispossessing the Alphans of their weapons and tossing them into a pile in the centre of the cavern. Yrcanos glowered at Frax, fixing him with an unnerving stare. 'You are nothing more than trash from the sewers of Skulnesh ...' Yrcanos began.

'Shut up!' Frax said nervously.

Yrcanos took a step nearer to the officer. 'You bring to the field of battle that which robs great warriors of their youth and virility. That is a crime against honour!'

Frax fingered the panel on his phaser. 'It was an

experiment conceived in the plague halls of Mogdana! And only a snivelling excuse like you would dare to use it as a weapon of disgrace against all that is noble ... Vroomnik!'

Yrcanos flung himself at Frax but the officer was too quick and the phaser spat a charge of energy that stopped Yrcanos in his rush. Silently the great warrior became transfixed, then crumpled into a lifeless heap. Seeing Yrcanos charge, Tuza had attempted to reach the arms pile, but then he, too, was gunned down.

Peri and the Lukoser tried to run but the weapons of the guards cut them down without mercy. They lay together, the girl and the Wolfman, a shaggy arm thrown across her in a futile last effort of protection.

'Are they dead?' the Doctor cried out across the courtroom.

'What does it look like?' the Valeyard said, his voice filled with cruel satisfaction.

Thirteen

'Is Peri dead?' the Doctor's question was directed to the Valeyard.

'That is difficult to answer precisely.'

'Then what was the point of showing that sequence?' the Inquisitor asked with a sharp edge to her question.

'Simply as further evidence of the Doctor's interference.'

'I thought it gratuitous.'

'And highly prejudicial! You won't convict me by using shock tactics.' The Doctor, feeling the Inquisitor to be favouring his case for once, tried to score as many points as possible.

The Valeyard remained unruffled. 'I require nothing so crude, my dear Doctor, all that will prove necessary is the plain, literal truth.'

'Then tell it!' the Doctor challenged.

'Enough of this bickering!' the Inquisitor said testily.

The Valeyard bowed in acquiescence. 'May we proceed with the evidence?'

'Indeed, Sagacity, we must.'

All heads turned to the screen where Frax was picking his way among the bodies of Peri, Yrcanos, Tuza and the Lukoser.

*

Yrcanos was the first to stir as the effects of the stunning force bolts began to wear off.

'Uhooh ... uh! My head feels as if it's been trampled by the seven-legged chargers of Corojaam,' Yrcanos groaned.

Peri was the next to stir. 'My legs, my arms ...'

'You are fortunate to be alive,' Frax said, looking down as the quartet regained consciousness.

Tuza stared up at the officer. 'So the Mentors can experiment with us?'

'Think of it as a community service, my dear Tuza.'

Yrcanos climbed to his feet flexing his legs painfully. 'You are a fool to leave us alive. I wouldn't have set the phasers to stun. Only kill. Kill.'

'That is because you are a barbarian.'

Peri tried to clear the painful throb of pain that was making a circular tour of her skull. 'You're some angel of mercy, huh, Frax?'

The officer became bored with the conversation. 'Get up. All of you!'

As they obeyed the order Peri asked, 'How did you know where we were?'

Frax shrugged. 'We have always known about the arms dump.'

'Liar!' Tuza accused the officer vehemently. 'You would have acted before now if you had!'

Frax regarded the group before him. His look shifted beyond them to the abject band of Alphan prisoners. 'Weapons are only as good as the training of the men that use them. You are no warrior, Tuza ...' Frax then turned a thumb to indicate Yrcanos. 'But him – now he's just enough in love with death to inspire rabble like yours into action. And we were right ... now move.'

Surrounded by guards who seemed anxious to

practise their expertise with phaser weapons, there was nothing any of the rebels could do but to move off – a dispirited band following a king whose eyes streamed with tears of humiliation at the dishonour of being made a prisoner.

'The sea ... the sea ... strong, strong, strong, too much ... too ... sting, sting, strike!'

Worriedly Crozier followed a scan of the mind of Lord Kiv. The Mentor leader continued to ramble incoherently as he lay under the examining lights that beamed down from above the operating table.

Sil was becoming more and more agitated. 'Why is the Lord Kiv talking of such things. He hates sea water.'

Crozier shook his head worriedly.

The Doctor walked across from behind the bank of computer heads and paused to look down at the babbling, feverish, Kiv. 'The body you transplanted Kiv's brain into, whose was it?'

'Just a body,' Crozier said.

'Bit casual that, isn't it?'

'I had no choice, Doctor, there are hardly any suitable donors.'

The Doctor moved to Crozier and viewed the scramble of erratic lines on the brain scan chart. 'Might have been better if you'd waited.'

'There wasn't time.'

The Doctor traced a random line of the VDU. 'Look at that – the host brain cells are trying to influence Kiv's implanted cortex. Attempting to alter and distort his memory.'

'A few must have escaped the laserisation.'

Unnoticed, Sil had been carried within earshot by his bearers. 'You have blundered, Crozier, you have

108

reduced the greatest business brain in the universe to a mere catcher of sea snakes!'

The Doctor became thoughtful, unmoved by Sil's bluster. 'Perhaps the trauma of the donor's death lingers and is infecting Kiv's brain.'

'I must try and rectify it – Matrona, increase the severin. Inject to four micro-sentiles.'

While the Matrona bent to make the adjustment to Kiv's life support system, Sil voiced his worries. 'There is an imminent summit meeting over which the Lord Kiv must preside. Our business partner from Sondlex might find it fishy should Lord Kiv be missing, gone insane.'

At the sound of his name Kiv opened his eyes. 'Have my briefing tapes and expansion strategy options been baited?'

'Er, not yet Magnificence.'

'Do it, or you shall be the first to sample the power of my new sting, Sil... I'm told... told...' Kiv's yellow eyes began to close. 'Told even a touch can... kill.'

'One micro-sentile more,' Crozier ordered.

The Matrona added a small increase of the life-giving fluid that alone was sustaining the existence of Kiv and everyone in the lab. The Mentor's edict that all should perish should he die still stood as an instruction to the armed guards who watched the rise and fall of Kiv's chest and gills as intently as those whose survival depended on keeping Kiv alive.

Sil addressed Crozier and his helpers. 'The Lord Kiv must not only be present at the meeting with our business partners but also be able to make sane decisions. If he cannot, you will all suffer.'

Crozier nodded with a show of confidence. 'He'll be there. Though whose body he will inhabit isn't yet certain. We must transfer Kiv's brain to someone else without delay.'

'Whose body?' Sil asked. There was no answer, though Crozier's eyes flickered in the direction of the Doctor for a brief moment.

The corridor that contained the punishment cells rang with the opening and closing of the iron grilles.

Gradually all the Alphan prisoners were confined, leaving only Yrcanos, Peri, Tuza and the Lukoser to be marched towards a cell that was double-barred.

'My head still aches,' Tuza remarked to no one in particular.

'Be grateful you still have a head,' Frax said from just behind.

A guard pulled the door open. It took three others to subdue Yrcanos but eventually he was thrust inside. Peri and the Lukoser could not see the point of resisting, as the corridor was by now full of guards. They stepped into the cell to join the King who glared with hatred at his captors through the bars of the cell.

'Scrrsongebrate!' he threatened.

As Tuza was about to enter the cell Frax tapped the Alphan on the shoulder. 'Not you.'

Before Tuza could ask why, he was hurried away under guard with Frax striding along behind. As Tuza was hustled along past the other cells cries of defiance began to be heard.

'Silence!' Frax yelled but the hubbub continued until a couple of guards set their phasers to stun and sent force bolts streaming into the crowded cells.

In the end cell Peri tried to squint down the corridor in an attempt to see what was happening. 'Why do they want Tuza?'

'Execution,' Yrcanos said, his tone was grim. 'One at a time, that's how it will be.'

'Oh.' Peri turned and leaned against the bars. She made a forlorn figure. Sensing her mood of dejection the Lukoser began to whine in sympathy which brought a swift kick from Yrcanos. The Lukoser yowled and rubbed his ribs before crouching down.

'What is it, my lady?' the King asked.

'Oh, it's just... ever since we came to Thoros-Beta I've been homesick, not so much for a place, but a time. I want to be back in my own time with people I love.'

'What is that? Love?'

Peri considered. 'When you care for something or someone more than yourself, I guess.'

The Lukoser lifted his head from where it was resting on his paws.

'M... more than yourself?'

'I know it sounds silly but sometimes more than life.'

'I care nothing for mine,' Yrcanos said.

'How can you say that, you're crazy as a loon!'

'I do not know what a loon is. On my planet of Krontep, if we die well our spirit is returned to life by being born into a more noble warrior.'

Peri could not follow the logic in the King's philosophy. 'Until what? Where are you going to end after all your brave deaths?'

'You become me – a King!' Yrcanos thumped his breastplate. 'After my next death, I will join the other Kings on Verduna, home of the Gods.'

'To do what?'

'Why, fight, what else?'

Peri began to laugh. 'That figures.' Then the laughter turned to tears.

*

Under the laboratory lights Tuza tried to remain calm. Steel restraining bands were fitted to his neck and forehead. The Doctor placed measuring calipers to various parts of Tuza's skull while the Matrona attached sensors to his temples.

Crozier looked at the resultant readings on the persona printout. 'These Alphan neural patterns are most unsuitable for Lord Kiv,' he said crossly.

The Doctor straightened, after completing his examination with the calipers, and said, 'The skull capacity is too great.'

Their disappointment was obvious to Frax who had been watching the various tests with interest.

Crozier turned to him. 'Was there anyone else?'

'Not amongst the Alphans, sir.'

The Matrona pointed at Tuza. 'Shall I have this one implanted and sent to the work sector?'

'Yes, yes . . .' Crozier had no further interest in the matter now that Tuza was eliminated as a possible donor for Kiv. 'Take him to the Induction centre.'

'Yes, Matrona.' Frax saluted and waited for Tuza to be released.

Crozier shook his head sadly as he and the Doctor tidied away their equipment and turned off the scanning equipment. 'What a pity both you and the Alphan are unsuitable, Doctor.'

The Doctor gave a slight swallow of disbelief at the matter-of-fact assumption Crozier made about his willingness to become a donor. 'Oh, yes,' he said lightly, 'most disappointing. Unlike Sil, I would willingly have given up my life.'

'Yes, of course.' Crozier's attention shifted momentarily as the door opened to allow Tuza to be taken away under guard. He turned back to the Doctor. 'What about

112

your companion, Doctor?'

'Peri?' The Doctor paused as if considering the matter carefully. 'Oh, female, quite unsuitable. Unstable. Silly. Flippety-gibbet, hopeless.'

'Why not examine her?' the Matrona suggested.

'Why not?' Crozier stared at the Doctor. 'You seem uneasy.'

'I would prefer someone else to be used.'

'You have strong feelings for the woman?'

'I would prefer it if someone else could be operated on instead.'

Crozier considered the question. After a long pause, he said, 'I understand. People have feelings. I am not without pity and you have helped me here. Kiv is stable. I can afford to allow him to gain strength for a few more hours. But I must operate on him again soon. Go to the Induction centre. You know what we need. If you can find a more suitable candidate, I shall use them and spare Peri.'

It amused Crozier to see how quickly the Doctor moved towards the exit from the laboratory. 'Hurry, Doctor, you have very little time . . . or chance,' he added for the Matrona's amusement, when the Doctor had gone.

Fourteen

The grille of the maximum-security cell slid open. The
guard pointed at Peri. The large hand of Yrcanos
touched the girl lightly on the shoulder. 'Die well.'

Peri looked up at him, eyes moist with tears. The
Lukoser began to growl menacingly. The guards hastily
grabbed Peri and pulled her from the cell. Yrcanos
gripped the steel bars, pulling with all his strength. Even
his power made no impression on their fixtures.

'Conzonian! Stizr! Azarapurr!'

The cries of a Krontep King's lament for a lost love
filled the underground passage with its sonorous
heartfelt cry of farewell. The Lukoser threw his head
back and howled angrily until even Yrcanos could stand
it no longer.

'Enough, Dorf, too much grief is unseemly, we will
meet the Lady Peri in Verduna.'

Yet somehow that did not seem a great comfort.
Yrcanos and the Lukoser slumped into a glum silence.

The Induction chamber was deserted except for Marne,
the aged Mentor with the over-sensitive hearing
problem.

'Where is everyone?' the Doctor asked.

'Don't shout; we are not expecting any intake from

114

Thoros-Alpha today.'

A suspicion flitted across the Doctor's mind. Had Crozier known this?

'Nobody at all?' the Doctor tried again.

'Only one subject in the Implantation cubicle.'

'Do you mind if I peek in, I do have Crozier's permission.'

'If you must, but he will probably be in the bemused stage by now.'

'I'll try not to disturb him.'

'Oh, all right,' Marne said, yawning.

'Thank you.' The Doctor went to the small cubicle and peered inside. Seated, and wearing a collar and helmet attachment that was wired to a persona reconstruction unit, was Tuza.

'Hello,' the Doctor started.

Tuza stared blearily at the indistinct features of the face swimming before him. 'Yrcanos?'

'You know him?'

'Yes. Who...'

'I'm a friend,' the Doctor said quietly and started to disengage the reconstruction unit to prevent any further damage to the Alphan's mind and spirit.

Expecting execution, Peri had at first been relieved to find herself taken to Crozier's laboratory, but as the tests on her person became more detailed she began to be apprehensive as to what might be in store for her. As the Matrona stepped back, from the examining table, Peri asked what was going on.

'Simply testing your state of health.'

'And?'

'It is excellent.'

'Good.' Peri sat up from the table.

'Yes. Most pleasing.'

At that moment the door opened and Crozier entered.

'Stand up!' the Matrona ordered. Peri left the table and stood silently by as Crozier scanned the sheet of figures and measurements taken by the Matrona.

Crozier kept glancing up at Peri as he read the print out. 'Yes ... oh, yes ... most promising.' He handed the information back to the Matrona and came towards Peri, smiling.

Peri watched him warily. She felt like a prize specimen as Crozier tilted her head first one way then the other.

'Excellent!' he pronounced. 'She is a most promising candidate. I will arrange the antigen tests.'

'That's a blood test,' Peri said with alarm. 'I'm not marrying anyone ...'

Crozier smiled indulgently. 'Spirit. Strength. That is good. We must try to retain that if at all possible.'

Tuza was slowly coming to himself but the Doctor, after examining the powerful mind-changing unit, knew that hours would be needed to recover his senses. At last the Doctor understood why he had suffered blackouts and had acted so perversely since he had suffered the power of Crozier's ability to warp minds. Though the Doctor had only felt the impulse of the Brain Transference Unit for a short time it had taken until now to recover his judgement fully. Deciding to allow Tuza more time to gather his wits the Doctor stepped outside the booth – just as Frax was arriving.

'What are you doing here, Doctor?' Frax asked.

'He has Crozier's permission and will you please not shout at each other.'

'My apologies, sir,' Frax said, recognising Marne, the oldest working Mentor. 'I didn't notice you were in attendance.'

'Oh, take no notice of me. Few people do.'

'I'm looking for that captured King ...' the Doctor said casually. 'Where might I find him?'

'Yrcanos?'

'That's him.'

'Why?'

'Crozier asked me to look him over as a possible body donor for Mentor Kiv.'

Frax hesitated then looked to Marne for approval.

'Oh, take him, but be careful – Yrcanos has a very loud voice ... it plays havoc with the audio system.'

'Thank you for the warning, Mentor,' the Doctor said quietly.

'I was hoping we'd heard the last of Yrcanos – he's such a strident fellow ...' The Mentor turned around to find himself alone. 'Oh, they've gone ... how rude not to say goodbye – young people.' He sniffed, closed his eyes and fell fast asleep.

Crozier showed the pattern of Peri's brain scan. 'Look at that, Matrona, so many positive waves ... I feel tempted to try for the ultimate experiment.'

'Another physical transfer?' The Matrona searched the scientist's face for a clue as to his intentions.

Crozier smiled like a small boy who is about to reveal his pet frog and just knows the girl will scream. Then he postponed his revelation. 'There are other tests to conduct first. Then I will decide. You may prepare the patient, even so, Matrona.'

'Yes, sir ...' the Matrona said, moving towards a bench on which was an open tray containing a selection of surgical scissors.

*

Propped against the back wall of his cell, Yrcanos was asleep, dreaming of a battle where warhorses clashed and fought, while warriors stood by and cheered. A rattling sound brought him awake. Standing outside the bars of the cell stood the Doctor and Frax. Without conscious thought Yrcanos was on his feet and hurling abuse at his enemies.

'Grunnitzer!'

'How do you do?' the Doctor said politely.

'Screedner!'

'Now where would a well-brought-up King learn such a word?' The Doctor turned to Frax. 'Open the door, please, officer, I intend to teach this king a royal lesson.'

'You must be out of your mind. He'll kill you!'

'Oh, I don't think so ...' the Doctor leaned towards Frax and deftly relieved him of the phaser that the officer carried in his belt.

'What ... ?' Frax started.

'No questions.' The Doctor levelled Frax's gun at Yrcanos.

'Grunwitzer!' Yrcanos bellowed defiantly.

'Enough of that,' the Doctor said, briskly. 'I'm here to help you. Officer Frax, please unlock the cell.'

Frax stared for a moment then took out the keys and unlocked the grille. The Doctor pulled the barred gate open. Yrcanos stood dazedly as if he had just received a sideswipe from a cannon ball.

'Your majesty ...' The Doctor waved an elegant gesture of invitation to quit his captivity.

Yrcanos made no move.

The Doctor nodded to the furry creature who had come to the shoulder of his master. 'Hello ... didn't catch your name at our last meeting.'

'Do ... do ... do ...'

'Never mind, you can tell me later.'

'His name is Dorf . . .' said Yrcanos suddenly, 'and you are scum!'

'Actually, I'm the Doctor. You don't have to thank me too effusively for helping you to escape . . . here, hold this . . .' The Doctor handed the phaser to Yrcanos. 'Now can we please move?'

Baffled, looking from the weapon thrust into his fist then at the Doctor, Yrcanos finally consented to leave the cell along with the Lukoser.

'Just a moment, officer . . .'

Frax did not hesitate to enter the cell. Steel bars between himself and Yrcanos seemed like an excellent idea. The Doctor locked Frax in then joined the King and his wolf-like companion.

'How . . . ?' Yrcanos started but the Doctor held up a hand.

'Later.'

'What?' Yrcanos puzzled as the Doctor went stepping out at speed away down the corridor.

'C'mon . . .' he muttered to an equally perplexed Dorf. 'Let's catch him up. Maybe we can get this Doctor to shut up long enough to allow us to kill him . . .'

The meeting between the Sondlex representatives was about to begin. Kiv bowed a welcome to the feathered chief negotiator. The turkey-red face grimaced and twittered a greeting in return. Other Mentors bowed in acknowledgement of the board members of Sondlex who settled down in a flutter of wings and flexing of talons.

Kiv's head drooped on to the translation box on his chest. Sil leaned forward and prodded him awake. 'You are unwell, Magnificence. You should not have left the shelter of Crozier's lab.'

119

'He has given me drugs to stabilise my condition and help me keep alert ... do you smell fish?'

'No, Magnificence, there is nothing of a fishy nature. My Lord ...' Sil hesitated, wondering how to raise the delicate matter of Kiv's irrational and erratic behaviour. 'I have the deepest respect for Crozier's skill but ...'

'But nothing, Sil. I must attend this meeting otherwise we could all finish up poor as fisherfolk. Now what is more important, my well-being or your wealth?'

Sil considered, then realised that there was no easy answer. 'That is a trick question, Magnificence, but can I say that if you feel well enough to cope with the negotiations, who am I to contradict?'

'Good.'

Kiv lay back on his chair suddenly disorientated. Flashes of pink seascapes kept coming to his mind. The waves would at first fascinate him but then bring a sudden nausea. It was most upsetting; still, Crozier had promised him a better home for his consciousness soon. There was that smell again – fish ... a green face crumpled with concern came before his eyes. 'Yes, Sil, what is it?' Kiv asked.

'All the council of Mentors are now present and the Sondlex Corporation are wondering ...'

'Let us begin, then,' Kiv said, banishing a vision of a sea snake rearing above the prow of a fishing smack.

King Yrcanos glowered at the Doctor's back. The situation was becoming intolerable to a man of honour. 'Doctor, I must know!' Yrcanos reached forward and turned the Doctor abruptly. 'I will not take another step until I am told the truth!'

'What truth?'

'Why did you release Dorf and myself?'

120

'I thought that would be obvious. I need your help to defeat the Mentors.'

'That I can understand. But you are my sworn enemy, Doctor. I have vowed to kill you!'

'Yes, well, we can sort all that out later. For the moment we need each other.'

The Lukoser's jaws began to open. 'He has a p ... po ... poi ...'

'Yes,' Yrcanos said, 'everyone seems to have a point nowadays. I am a man of action not nit-picking reason!'

'You'll see plenty of action.'

The King looked long and hard at the Doctor while the Lukoser scratched an ear. Finally the pugnacious angle of the black beard lessened. 'Then lead on, Doctor, but first we must find my bride-to-be.'

'Yrcanos, we haven't time for you to go courting.'

'I am talking of the Earth woman, Perpugilliam of the Brown.'

'Oh, that one ... is she aware of your nuptial intentions?'

'That is unimportant. As a mere female, she is like a fortress – to be taken by storm! Her consent is quite unnecessary.'

'Some fortresses never surrender.' The Doctor paused. 'Come on, we'll look for Peri on the way.'

'But she m ... may ... be ... d ... d ... dead ... she and T ... Tuza ... were exec ... exec ...'

'Executives?'

'Executed,' Yrcanos corrected the Doctor.

'No. Tuza lives, we must get back to him now ... c'mon, Yrcanos – you too, c'mon, boy, I mean, Dorf ...'

'Guard! Guard!' Frax's cries finally attracted the attentions of a passing jailor.

'Get this door open. Yrcanos has escaped.'

Peri looked up at the dazzling battery of lights above the table which Crozier had insisted she occupy during a long series of further tests. A figure came between the lights and bent down to her. It was difficult to move with the tubes and wires attached to sensors that adhered to her forehead.

'Crozier?' Peri narrowed her eyes trying to focus upon the identity of her examiner.

'Yes.'

'Am I fit and healthy?'

'Perfectly.'

Peri pressed her hands to the table ready to sit up but this proved impossible due to restraining clamps that had been quietly placed about her neck and shoulders. 'Hey!' Peri protested.

'Lie there and rest, Peri, all my tests are complete. You are a perfect specimen, perfect. Yes ...' Crozier allowed himself the luxury of looking at the girl laid out along the operating table. 'Matrona, you may inform the Lord Kiv that I am ready to conduct my ultimate experiment.'

Fifteen

The aged Mentor sat on his stool and nodded sleepily over his console while across the chamber the Doctor, Yrcanos and the Lukoser surveyed the empty Induction chamber and the guard who now stood outside the cubicle.

'Is Tuza inside that devil box?' Yrcanos whispered.

'Yes.'

'I shall obliterate the Mentor.' Yrcanos fiddled with the phaser's power setting.

'No. We'll try it my way first. I'm not going to let you cause a blood bath, give me that . . .' The Doctor held out his hand for the energy weapon.

Yrcanos frowned, hesitated. 'You think like a warrior, but you do not act like one. You are a strange being, Doctor. Here . . .' Grudgingly Yrcanos handed the phaser across to the Doctor.

'Thank you. Now, Dorf, you remain here and you, your Majesty, behave yourself and follow me.' Cautiously the Doctor and the Warlord began to advance on the drowsing Mentor. They made an eye-catching pair with the Doctor's coat of many colours and the white garb and gold inlaid breastplate and shiny black helmet of the warlord.

Some paces away from the Mentors' workspace

Marne came awake, his acute hearing warning of their soft approach. He turned to greet his visitors. 'Ah, Doctor, I see you have found your clamorous King.'

'Yes ... yes ...' The Doctor and Yrcanos drifted towards the armed guard who barred their way from entering the cubicle where Tuza was, hopefully, by now recovered from his interrupted induction treatment. 'My intention is to shut the King up for good and all.'

'Oh, good ...' The Mentor smiled with toothless gums.

'Yes,' the Doctor continued, now almost within reach of the guard, 'I thought I'd implant one of those brain control things.'

'Oh, for one pleasurable moment I thought you were going to kill him. I presume you have Crozier's permission to carry out the experiment.'

'Oh, absolutely,' the Doctor said. 'He's given me a free hand where the good King is concerned.'

'Oh, really?' The wizened face expressed its owner's disapproval by a downward rearrangement of the cracks and crevices. 'I wish Crozier would keep me abreast of events. He has no idea how much paperwork his irregular activities create.' Marne activated a screen.

'What are you doing?' the Doctor asked, politely.

'I shall have to get confirmation of just how free a hand Crozier has given you.'

The Doctor looked at Yrcanos who instantly chopped a hand to the neck of the guard who blinked once and then collapsed into insensibility. At the same time the Doctor stabbed a 'clear' switch which temporarily prevented Marne clearing a line into the laboratory. The Mentor reached for an alarm circuit but hesitated a vital second, fearing the noise that it would make.

Yrcanos bounded across and placed a hand on the arm

of Marne, preventing a switch from being depressed. 'Be still, old one, unless you wish your wizened existence terminated.'

'All right,' Marne sighed with relief. 'Thank you.'

'For your life?'

'No, for not shouting.'

When Tuza saw the Doctor enter the cubicle he tried to rouse himself and succeeded, with the Doctor's help, on raising himself and stumbling out into the Induction chamber.

On seeing the Alphan leader, Yrcanos saluted with clenched fist across his breastplate. 'My friend! We both live. Now to drench this world with the blood of our enemies!'

The Mentor clapped his hands to his ears. 'Why must you yell such nauseating comments?'

Yrcanos chuckled and tickled the Mentor's chin. 'Be quiet, wrinkled one, otherwise you'll be the first to die. How is Tuza, Doctor?'

'All right, I hope. The implant has not taken. I must have stopped the process just in time.'

'What is this implant devilry?'

'Are you shouting that question at me?' the Mentor asked.

'Yes ...' Yrcanos said.

'One of Crozier's newer developments. More paperwork, of course, but we've been having problems with some of the Alphan slaves. The implant helps impede any fractious or rebellious thoughts. A little implant dart in the base of the neck and every Alphan is a good one.'

Yrcanos and the Doctor both remembered the burntout specimens they had stumbled on with Tuza. 'Where is the control point for this process?' Although the question was raised casually there was an undertone of grim determination beneath the words.

'Oh, I wouldn't know that,' Marne said hastily.

'Come on, withered one or ...'

'I know where it is,' Tuza said suddenly.

'Then let's go ...' the Doctor said.

Yrcanos frowned. 'To release slaves? I had envisaged a more noble cause for which to fight.'

'Think of the chaos if we can remove the mind control the Mentor's have over the Alphans,' the Doctor said as the Lukoser padded across the chamber towards their group. Yrcanos seemed unconvinced about helping the Alphans. The Doctor tried another tack.

'Think about it, Yrcanos, the slaves, once released could supply you with a very willing army.'

'He's right,' Tuza said.

'Silence!' Yrcanos roared, which caused Marne to fall from his perch with the shock. 'I am King Yrcanos of the Krontep. I am more than capable of making my own decision!'

'Then please hurry,' said Marne, climbing back on to his stool, his ears still throbbing from the impact of the roaring voice of Yrcanos.

'Gu ... gu ... gua ...' the Lukoser started to try and say.

'Spit it out, Dorf,' ordered Yrcanos, thumping his equerry on the back.

'A patrol is coming,' the Lukoser said.

'Vroomnik!' the warcry resounded and reverberated.

'Aaah!' the Mentor covered his ears and spun round and round on his stool as the King stamped up and down.

'Doctor, let us release the slaves. And then let us battle unto glorious death!'

As Yrcanos started to storm away, the Doctor halted

the Mentor's spinning stool. 'Sorry about all the noise but he so loves his warrior work.'

'Just go. Just go,' Marne said weakly, one ear ringing and the other pounding in protest from the assault on his inner ear by the booming voice of Yrcanos.

'You won't do anything silly, will you?' the Doctor asked. 'Such as sounding an alarm.'

'My head is ringing like a bell tower. I have no intention of making it worse by setting off alarms – leave, please ...'

As the Doctor and Tuza hurried after Yrcanos and the Lukoser, the guard, who had been feigning unconsciousness for some time, jumped up and pressed a button. A siren began to wail with piercing shrillness.

'Sadist!' the Mentor cried, cowering under his console, trying to escape from the unremitting assault of the alarm hooter on his hearing.

The snip-snip of the scissors continued to make inroads into Peri's dark luxuriant hair. Soon great clumps fell on to the operating table. Unable to move her head, Peri had tried to protest, question, plead. All without any success. The Matrona went on with the cutting.

'Hey, that's skin ... you'll be down to my scalp soon.'

'That's the idea,' the Matrona said. She began to sweep the hair clippings away.

Crozier came across to examine the almost bald Peri. 'Shave the skull.'

'Yes, sir ...'

'What!' Peri shrieked.

'Quiet!'

Crozier stared down at Peri. His almost colourless eyes reflecting an intensity of thought. Then he relaxed as he decided on a course of action. 'Yes, Matrona, shave her head close, I have decided to attempt direct transference. Inform Kiv that all is ready.'

The sound of the alarm hooter receded behind them. Yrcanos, intent on reaching the Mind Control Centre of the Mentors, was leading the others along at a good pace when, without warning, a guard came through a doorway further down the passage. With surprising swiftness the guard produced a phaser and fired at them. The bolt sped towards Yrcanos who raised his arms and awaited its impact. At the last second the Lukoser hurled himself in front of his master. The charge of the phaser caught the Lukoser side on. He pitched forward with a cry of pain.

'What!' Yrcanos cried and fired at the retreating guard. His shot hit their attacker between the shoulders causing him to stagger and collapse in the doorway of the chamber.

'Advance!' Yrcanos waved his companions on while he knelt beside his dying equerry. He could see the gaping wound in the Wolfman's side. 'There is no more noble end than to intercept the destiny of another's death. You will be granted a princely return.'

'I am pleased to die. I would no longer wish to live like this ... half beast ... half ...' The Lukoser's wolf head sagged. The eyes filmed over. Yrcanos made the blessing ritual for a dead Kontrep warrior: a complicated pattern of crosses and salutes that ended with his head bowed over his dead equerry.

The Doctor and Tuza burst through the door of Induction Control. Facing them were five armed guards. The officer in charge of the guards was known to them.

'I somehow knew you would finish up here,' Frax

said.

'You were right for once,' the Doctor said. 'Where is Peri?'

'I believe she is with Crozier.'

'That's what I feared.'

Frax jerked the phaser weapon towards the door. 'Now move. Mentor Sil will be delighted to have his suspicions confirmed about you, Doctor.'

'I bet.' As they moved between the banks of computer monitors, with an escort of two guards and Frax, the Doctor spoke to Tuza as if in casual conversation, hoping that Yrcanos would be lurking somewhere nearby. 'Have you met Sil?'

'No,' Tuza replied.

'Sil has a very high opinion of himself. Constantly munches Marsh Minnows ...'

They were bustled out into the corridor. Warily the guards checked in each direction. Nothing unusual seemed apparent. Even the mist for once had cleared.

'Move!' Frax dug the phaser into the Doctor's back.

The Doctor pretended not to notice but moved, with Tuza alongside him, and continued his conversation with as much naturalness as he could manage in the circumstances. 'Sil ... yes, his morals are as fishy as his eating habits. What a creature to have officiating at one's execution ...'

'He won't have us put to death. We'll be implanted as slaves,' Tuza replied his eyes roaming the passageway.

Where was Yrcanos?

They turned a corner and saw, a dozen paces ahead of them, the body of the Lukoser. Two of the guards went to examine the corpse, leaving Frax behind to cover Tuza and the Doctor.

'Dead, sir ...' one of the guards started to say when he

was interrupted by a mighty roar from above.

'Vroomnik!' yelled Yrcanos as he leapt down from his hiding place in the crevice above them. Felling Frax with a blow that would have splintered an oak tree, Yrcanos then bounded towards the two guards and threw a giant arm about each of their necks and crushed their skulls together like a cook cracking eggs. Yrcanos let the two guards fall to join the Lukoser on the floor of the corridor.

'Dorf is dead,' Yrcanos said, quietly.

'I'm sorry,' the Doctor said, sympathetically.

Yrcanos shook his head. 'He died fighting ... it was an honourable death.'

Tuza, overcome by the swiftness of their rescue, began to recover his wits. 'I, too, am sorry about your friend, Yrcanos, but we must destroy the slave control.'

Yrcanos looked up from contemplating Dorf; in his eyes, the fire of revenge brightened.

'Lead me to it. I demand the privilege of initiating the demise of the Mentors!'

'The Doctor is on the rampage with that mad King Yrcanos, Magnificence ...'

'Is that any reason to interrupt an important conference?'

Sil spoke in a whisper to avoid the straining ears of the Sondlex negotiation team that fluttered and trilled amongst themselves at this unexpected break in the grain-bartering process.

'They are very dangerous, Magnificence, they could cause a great deal of damage.'

'That is nothing to what you are doing to my negotiations. If I'm not careful, I could lose an important fish dish.'

'But you hate fish, Magnificence.'

'Do I?' Kiv became confused. Sil decided to acquaint Kiv with Crozier's proposal for a permanent solution to his problems of mental clarity. Kiv listened with growing excitement. 'What chances of success, Sil?'

'Good.'

Kiv hesitated, put all visions of baby sea snake out of his mind and addressed the delegates. 'I am unable to accept your proposals. I must insist that our agreement to purchase grain from you remain at the previous price for a further quarter. Then any future agreement will be made restrospective. Now excuse me. I must sail to a safer harbour.' Sil signalled to Kiv's bearers and then to his own.

Soon the two Mentors were carried from the conference chamber away from the angry buzzing and twittering of the Sondlexians towards the laboratory where Kiv hoped a dramatic transformation to his mind and body would be achieved.

Peri was laid out on the operating table like a sacrificial victim. She was pleased about one thing only – she could not see herself with her shaven skull. She lay clamped and wired ready for whatever terrifying experiment Crozier and the Matrona were planning.

'All is ready.' The Matrona indicated Peri. 'We only need Kiv.' Crozier looked distracted. 'This time you will succeed, sir.'

'This time could be my last time for anything. But yes, no time for doubt. We will ... what ...?'

The lights of the laboratory had dimmed momentarily.

'Find out what is happening,' Crozier's voice filled with urgency as the power supply faltered again. 'Should power fail during the transference operation, life will be over for all of us!'

Sixteen

'Raaaghner!' Yrcanos yelled exultantly from among the wreckage of consoles and computer terminals that moments before had controlled the minds and attitudes of the Alphan slave population. 'Now not only will the legends sing of Yrcanos the great warlord but also of the great liberator!'

Tuza stepped over their fallen enemies and joined the Doctor who was ensuring that all control centre circuits were damaged beyond repair.

'Yrcanos is certainly a man of little modesty.'

'Yes, we'd better halt his self eulogy.'

'Hey, it's time to find your warrior queen, isn't it?'

Yrcanos smote himself on his war helmet which rang out in reverberation at the blow. 'Of course, I need the Lady Peri to grace my moment of triumph!'

Throughout the domain of the Mentors Alphans were reacting with confusion to their sudden liberation. Until their reason could readjust to reality chaos would be inflicted on the rule of the Mentors. Sil and Kiv, being borne along towards Crozier's laboratory, found themselves faced by a group of Alphan slaves milling about and blocking their progress.

'What's going on ...?' Sil cried from the safety of his

chair. 'Why all this confusion? Out of the way – his Magnificence is unwell!'

Bracing themselves, the Mentors' bearers began to shoulder their way through the bewildered throng. Swaying dangerously and clinging to their chairs above the madness, Sil panicked while Kiv merely smiled and observed that the sea was certainly rough today. On hearing this Sil decided Kiv must have treatment right away. A pair of Alphans cannoned into Sil's throne, almost causing him to capsize. Sil screamed out, fear giving stridency to his voice, 'Careful, profitless fools! Is it not enough that one great leader suffers seasickness without threatening the life of another!'

Thrusting and kicking the Alphans aside, finally the bearers forced their way through and attained the haven of the passageway that led towards Crozier's laboratory.

The Matrona, peering out fearfully, saw Sil and Kiv and came anxiously to meet them. 'Anarchy has broken out,' she said as Crozier came out of the laboratory to join her.

'What's happening out there?'

Sil grimaced. 'Just a few thousand servants going mad! And good riddance I say! All they do is eat you out of house and home!' Kiv, from behind Sil, began to sob uncontrollably.

Crozier went to examine the leader of the Mentors. After a moment of deliberation he reached his decision. 'Kiv is deteriorating. I must operate. Prepare Kiv and the girl at once!'

After their moment of liberation, panic then made the mass of Alphans want to escape from the underground world of the Mentors. Trying to reach the laboratory of Crozier, in order to free Peri, the Doctor and his group

133

found it difficult to progress against the tide of Alphan servants and workers who were running under a desperate compulsion to reach the open air.

'Clear the way ... I must find my lady!' Yrcanos shouted, thrusting bodies aside as he headed through the stream of fleeing Alphans.

Tuza, sheltering behind the king as much as he could, assumed the Doctor was close up behind him. But, unnoticed by Tuza or Yrcanos, a baffling phenomena was taking place – an unremitting force was dragging the Doctor backwards. Try as he might the Doctor could do nothing to resist the mysterious power that swept him away from the main throng and into a side passage.

With a sudden trumpeting sound the TARDIS appeared; the door opened. The Doctor, helpless to resist, was drawn inside. The door closed. The TARDIS began to dematerialise. Soon the passage was empty of the TARDIS which, taken out of time, was spinning down a white shaft of light.

In the courtroom the Doctor, like the rest of the Time Lords, averted his eyes from the brilliance of the light that shone from the Matrix screen. 'I remember now ... I remember!' The flood of light pouring from the screen lessened. The words burst on the assembled Time Lords. 'Whatever made you take me out of time when you did? I remember it all! How I only pretended to help the Mentors. I was on my way to save Peri!'

The Inquisitor spoke authoritively. 'Things had gone too far, you had released chaos and allowed your companion to take part in an experiment that would affect all future life in the universe!'

'I did try to stop it,' the Doctor said, his voice bitter and stubborn.

'But you could not succeed. It was too late and therefore necessary, under the direct order of the High Council, to prevent the consequence of Crozier's experiment.'

The Inquisitor turned to the screen. 'I suggest you watch this final sequence most carefully, Doctor.'

The Matrix activated and the final act of the tragic adventure began.

'A perfect transfer,' the Matrona completed her final neural readings. Crozier nodded. He seemed dazed at the accomplishment of his life's dream.

'I believe we have altered the basis of all future life.'

Sil was staring at the two inert bodies that lay on adjoining tables. Both Peri and Lord Kiv both seemed dead to him. 'Kiv's brain is inside the head of that repulsive Earth being?'

Crozier smiled at Sil's lack of understanding. 'No. I have achieved much more than that – I have transferred only the contents of Kiv's mind into the brain of the woman.'

'Sir ...' The Matrona indicated that the body of the girl was beginning to stir.

'Thank you, Matrona. We will soon see if we have been over optimistic.'

'What of the Earth woman's mind?' Sil asked.

'Quite gone. Mentally she no longer exists.'

A slow dawn of understanding began to glimmer inside the crafty brain of Sil. 'And you can transfer any mind into any body?'

'Yes. When the Earth woman's brain ages, I can transfer the mental energy and consciousness of Lord Kiv on to yet another body. He need never die!'

Sil bounced up and down; from his mouth bubbled a

froth of excitement at the prospect stretching before him. 'Immortality!' he cried in ecstasy.

Tuza and Yrcanos looked up and down the mist-shrouded corridor. 'Now where?' the Warlord asked.

'Around the next corner.'

'Good.' Yrcanos checked the automatic phaser he was carrying – it was a more developed model with greater fire capacity and range than the usual hand weapon. 'I shall enjoy destroying Crozier.'

Tuza was not paying attention but kept glancing behind him as if expecting someone to join them. 'What are you looking for, Tuza, phantoms?'

'Do you not have the feeling something's missing?'

'No.' Yrcanos began to move off.

Tuza hurried to join him. 'It was as though there was someone else here just a minute ago ... that there were three of us.'

Yrcanos clapped Tuza on the shoulder and grinned. 'You sense the presence of Milda, the great god of war. That is good. It seems I will make a warrior out of you yet ... wait!' Through the mist a figure loomed. Yrcanos thrust the automatic phaser out ready to blast away.

'Wait!' Tuza said as a bewildered Alpha woman servant tottered toward them.

'What must I do?' she beseeched Tuza.

'Go and find others like you – go with them – soon you will see the world clearly again.'

'Thank you ... thank you ...' the woman said and wandered away.

Yrcanos nodded in approval. 'A leader must care for his people while he lives. He must also be prepared to die for them – look!'

Tuza peered round the corner. Down the next

corridor a red light glared above the entrance to Crozier's laboratory. Two guards stood on sentry both outside.

'Only two guards – the gods are with us.'

'What do we do?' Tuza breathed.

Yrcanos grinned. 'Two guards – two of us. We engage in combat – like true warriors!'

Tuza stared uneasily at Yrcanos whose eyes were ablaze with the onset of fighting madness. 'What exactly does that . . . ?' Tuza started to ask but Yrcanos erupted into action.

'Frontal attack! Naardra!' The charge of Yrcanos was launched with a less enthusiastic Tuza being dragged along in the tail of the hurricane. But inexplicably, the attack did not maintain its savage momentum. Instead of bounding down the corridor to death or glory, the movements of the two attackers became slower and slower until they finally became two statues frozen in static time.

The colour intensity of the Matrix screen became harsher. 'They are caught in a time bubble,' the Inquisitor explained to the jury. 'Everything had to be perfect before they could be allowed to drive home their final attack.'

The Doctor pointed at the Inquisitor accusingly. 'You're using Yrcanos as an assassin!'

'It was judged by the High Council as the most acceptable way to resolve matters, Doctor. Yrcanos will never know that he was used.'

The Doctor looked with disgust at the Inquisitor, the jury and finally at the Valeyard. His look was contemptuous, his voice was bitter. 'And so they took it upon themselves to act like second-rate gods!'

*

137

The body of Peri raised itself to a sitting position. The shaven skull reflected a sheen from the lights above. A voice came from between the lips – although it was recognisable as a female voice, there was a resonance that hinted at the alien presence. The tone of the voice was expressive of a sense of wonder. Crozier, the Matrona and Sil began to listen with a sense of growing awe as Kiv began to experience the sensations of his new body.

'Warm, not cold ... the body is warm ... wonderful! Toes – wriggly toes. Legs. Trunk. Neck. A neck ... strong ... a head free of pain. Eyesight. Colours. I like this. Warm blood inside. Now I am she ... alive within this so wonderful warm frame.' The eyes that had once belonged to Peri glanced sidewards and down on to the crumpled reptilean shape on the next table.

'Ugh! That cold blooded reptile ... must die!'

'It already has, my lord, welcome to your new body.' Crozier said.

Sil wrinkled his nose as he contemplated his master's new appearance. 'I wish you could have found a more attractive carcass for my lord to occupy.'

The bubble of time that held Yrcanos and Tuza began to dissolve and the duo began to move slowly at first but then, within two strides, the King gained momentum. The guards heard the pounding feet, turned and started to level their guns. They were a beat of time too late. Yrcanos was upon them, scattering both with successive jabs of the phaser butt. With his ultimate warcry, 'Shoomvwy!' he thrust open the door of Crozier's laboratory.

Sil's bearers rushed to protect their master but Yrcanos fired and brought them down immediately. Another force bolt smashed Sil's water tank, sending the

138

terrified Mentor crashing down from his throne to thresh about in a paroxysm of utter terror. The body that Yrcanos thought was Peri rose imperiously from the table.

Her voice was harsh and brutal with command. 'Protect me! I am your lord and master!'

Confusion and disbelief chased across the face of Yrcanos. He looked first at Peri then at the body of Kiv beside her. Then horror of the truth penetrated to the soul of King Yrcanos. 'No!' he cried with anguish before he made himself point the nozzle of the phaser at what had once been the woman he loved. The phaser began to fire incessantly until the travesty of life was no more.

'You killed Peri!'

The Inquisitor was stunned by the carnage they had witnessed a moment before. She took some time to manage a reply. 'We had to act,' she said, finally. 'With the discovery Crozier had made the whole course of natural evolution throughout the universe would have been affected.'

'You killed Crozier, too?'

'It was necessary.'

The Valeyard rose to his feet, an austere ascetic figure wrapped in black robes. 'But Peri died, Doctor, because you abandoned her. We had to end her life because your negligence had made it impossible for her to live.'

'Lies!' The Doctor tried to hold on to his composure. He could best serve Peri by exposing the conspiracy that was ranged against him. 'The High Council had no right to order Peri's or anyone else's death.'

'Please, Doctor.'

'I was taken out of time for another reason .. and I have every intention of finding out what it is!'

The Valeyard smiled sardonically. 'That is something for the final section of the prosecution – the future. Doctor, we have seen you active in the far past. As to your recent activities – we have just witnessed your ineptitude. We had no choice but to extract you from the consequences of your dangerous meddling.'

The Doctor ignored the Valeyard and addressed an appeal to the Inquisitor. Waves of grief were coursing through him at the loss of Peri. 'I have seen my errors, my Lady, I will change. I promise.'

'No, Doctor, you do *not* change.' The Valeyard interjected before the Inquisitor could respond. 'Sagacity, I will demonstrate that in a possible future the Doctor continued to be the same interfering destroyer of the delicate fabric of time.'

The Inquisitor sighed. 'Will this take long, Valeyard?'

'Yes, Sagacity, I'm afraid it will.'

'Then I will declare a recess. After which the trial of the Doctor will continue.'

Seventeen

The court had emptied, leaving the Doctor alone with only the court bailiff for company. The Doctor stared blindly ahead trying to come to terms with the death of Peri. He had no way of knowing, then, that the High Council had exercised mercy and distorted the timeflow of the Matrix and extracted Peri and Yrcanos before the brain transfer operation. The odd pair had been transported through time and space back to Earth in the early part of the last decade of the twentienth century.

Peri was delighted to be back in her native country. Yrcanos, though happy enough to be with Peri, often complained that life in California was endlessly perplexing; to which Peri would reply that yes, it was, but he coped better than most barbarians who lived on the west coast of America.

When last seen Yrcanos had embarked on a career as an all-in wrestler, fighting under the title of Yrcanos, 'King of the Krontep', with Peri as his manager. His all-action style soon attracted a growing army of fans. Taking their name from his favourite warcry, his followers styled themselves 'Vroomniks' and were a most enthusiastic throng. Sitting in the crowd, Peri sometimes wondered what had befallen the Doctor; fortunately, her memories of Thoros-Beta were now mercifully vague and her future with Yrcanos, in her own time and country, made her quite content with the destiny the Time Lords had decreed for her.